PRAISE FOR *THE HOUSE ON GENESIS ROAD*

"*The House on Genesis Road* is an emotional reminder to live in the moment, soaking up every single second, openly, without masks or regrets. It spoke to my heart about the power of human relationships, and reminded me not to miss people put in my path because of distractions and fear. It also reminded me that, though we may feel lonely, we are never alone. We are connected ever so elegantly to the universe and those who have come before us. I could not put the book down."
—REBECCA BANDY, attorney at law

"If you decide to read this book, I suggest you set aside ample time to read it in one sitting. If not, you will miss several appointments that day as you won't be able to put it down."
—DANIEL WHITEMAN, PH.D.,
Vice Chairman, Coastal Construction Company

"A story of everlasting love and the devotion of a husband and father. When you finish, you should have a better understanding of how to spend the rest of your days."
—ROBERT C. JOSEFSBERG, husband, father, attorney at law

THE HOUSE ON GENESIS ROAD

A Never-Ending Love Story

Paul R. Lipton

Mulberry Harbor Press

LONGMONT, COLORADO

Paul Lipton / Mulberry Harbor Books
1818 Lombardy Street
Longmont , CO. 80503

Publisher's Note: This is a work of fiction. Names, characters, places, and incidents are a product of the author's imagination. Locales and public names are sometimes used for atmospheric purposes. Any resemblance to actual people, living or dead, or to businesses, companies, events, institutions, or locales is completely coincidental. The author of this work does not claim to give medical or mental health advice. If you suspect that you have a medical or mental health problem, we urge you to seek competent medical help.

Library of Congress Control Number 2022923226

The House on Genesis Road/ Paul R. Lipton. —1st ed.
ISBN 978-0-9890910-6-0 (paperback)
ISBN 978-0-9890910-7-7 (ebook)

To Margie, Melissa, and Lindsay

"Life itself is the most wonderful fairy tale."
HANS CHRISTIAN ANDERSON

"Morning, without you, is a dwindling dawn."
EMILY DICKINSON

"Each night, when I go to sleep, I die. And the next morning, when I wake up, I am reborn."
MOHANDAS K. GANDHI

CONTENTS

THE HOUSE ON GENESIS ROAD

1. The Sunrise

The house on Genesis Road sits quiet and unoccupied now.

The only house at the end of a sleepy dead-end street, the couple who lived there until four months ago named the road when they bought the property. Behind the house is an open field filled with wildflowers that is visited only by occasional wandering deer and bears looking for food and shelter.

Behind the open field sits the Bridger Range, which is part of the Rocky Mountains in southern Montana. In the range, the Sacajawea Peak, at 9,839 feet, used to be the husband's focal point for meditative moments, either in the early morning or in the evening at sunset, when he would stand at the railing on the deck with a mug of coffee or a glass of wine.

The man was the early riser. His wife would usually join him about a half hour into his first cup of coffee. They started each morning clicking their coffee cups together to toast the new day. At sunset they would continue this ritual by raising their glasses of wine to say how grateful they were to not only have this day but also have the day with each other.

They always commented on how they were blessed to live in this beautiful setting. They also would marvel at all the butterflies that graced their property. The man once commented that he felt like all his loved ones who passed on watched over the family through the multicolored butterflies.

In the early years of their retirement, when their golden retriever, Rembrandt, was still young and frisky, the dog would chase after squirrels and groundhogs. He was smart enough to leave the deer and bears alone. When Rembrandt was twelve years old, he just wore out. That was over ten years ago. The couple buried his ashes by an evergreen tree in the back. They put a small headstone over the grave that read: "Rembrandt filled our lives with humor, fun, color, beauty, and most of all, magic."

They never had another dog.

Because the back of the house faces west, the sunsets the couple saw were beyond breathtaking. Each sunset was different and always inspiring. As the man stood there beside his wife, it always felt to him like anything was possible. He truly believed and had the feeling that God was always present watching over them.

The couple had raised two daughters in the house. Their girls, Sarah and Rachel, grew up and moved away when it was time to go to college, but his memories of them in childhood lingered in his mind long after they were gone. The man had a dry riverbed dug midway between the house and the foothills of the mountain range. When it rained or snowed, this filled with water and then came alive with the sounds of the animals drinking from it. He loved remembering how his little girls used to skip back and forth over the wooden bridge he had built so they could cross the water.

Life in retirement was sweet. There was a gentleness to the day. The man and woman lived about fifteen miles from another house or store. Although this required them to plan wisely in regard to stocking up on groceries and other supplies, they loved the remoteness. Their property was their little slice of heaven, a Noah's Ark in the sea of the world's current unrest and upheaval. They rarely turned on the TV or visited the internet, except for chatting remotely with their daughters. Instead, they spent most of the time listening to music, playing games, and reading. The house was usually filled with the sounds of either guitar or piano instrumentals broadcast via speakers located throughout the house and on the back deck.

The woman was an avid reader of spy novels and murder mysteries—stories featuring a secret agent or quirky investigative lead character. She would devour one or two of these a week in between her regular excursions to the gym in town and keeping up with her gardening. The couple built a greenhouse in back where she grew all the vegetables the couple ate for lunch and dinner.

Her husband liked to read and study different philosophies. Whether it was *The Bhagavad Gita, The Bible,* or the writings of Marcus Aurelius, Rumi, and Gandhi, he would get lost in the poetry, mysticism, and wisdom of these books. Since college, he had enjoyed the study of ancient history, religion, and philosophy. Because it seemed clear to him that all people begin and end in the same place, he always hoped to one day understand why everyone had become so ideologically divided. *What drives our divides?* he wondered.

His curiosity always came back to the why for him. The why behind all we choose to do or *not*-do. He speculated, *What makes some go so bad while others strive to reinforce the good in all things?* He would read, make notes, and then reflect on how best to navigate the day and live a life endowed with some meaning and purpose.

It seemed appropriate, and almost divine, to choose to make the address of the house be 1318 Genesis Road. The couple believed they were endowing their domicile with a sacred purpose.

Genesis 13:18 is a verse in *The Bible.* The connection between their house and this verse gave him a sense of sanctuary and connection to place.

No matter what version of *The Bible* you read, whether King James, New International, or any other version, the message is the same.

> *"Then Abram removed his tent, and came and dwelt*
> *in the plain of Mamre, which is in Hebron, and built*
> *there an altar to the Lord."*
> GENESIS 13:18

The house on Genesis Road deserves a deeper introduction. It was itself an important part of the couple's unfolding story. The magic of the house was how it could comfort them in trying times and embraced them each evening.

A ranch-style house, sprawling across one level, the floor plan includes a massive living room. That was the one overarching requirement the couple expressed to their architect when the house was being designed. They wanted this living room to be at least forty by thirty square feet.

The back wall of the house is composed of all-glass doors and windows from ceiling to floor. These doors can slide open so the outside and inside are one. When the girls were young, they toasted marshmallows and made s'mores while they sat and told tall tales around a stone fire pit on the deck. There is also a two-sided fireplace in the middle of the living room with enough seating around it for moments with the whole family to occur—whether happy or sad. The construction of the indoor fireplace matches the outdoor fire pit on the deck.

There is a master bedroom where the couple slept, of course, and each of their daughters had her own room. On the opposite side of the house, there was a big recreation room furnished with a pinball machine and a ping pong table. When the girls were little, family ping pong or pinball contests would go on for hours some nights. The giggling of the girls was contagious. The family kept a yellow legal pad and pencil hanging from the pinball machine to keep track of the scores and see who, that week, was the new champion that the rest of the family had to try to defeat. This was serious business. It would make the man smile. After the girls got older and became more active beyond the home with friends their own ages, he missed those family evenings.

The kitchen had stools around the oversized countertop where quick meals and snacks were eaten. Sometimes the countertop and stools were where the man would sit, late into the night, after the girls and his wife were already asleep, and journal his thoughts of the day. His journals filled a whole shelf on the book and knickknack shelves in the master closet. Each page in the journals started with the date and the time, and then reflected his hopes and dreams of the day to come.

While his wife was doing her gardening, reading, or studying feng shui (which became her obsession), the man was in his "cave," the den. That was his quiet spot. Furnished with an oversized, overstuffed leather reclining chair, this was his secluded private island on a Saturday evening where he would read and write while his wife, more than likely, was either putting a new plant in some corner of the house to redirect the flow of energy in that spot or on the phone catching up with family and friends. His wife, after all, was the glue that kept everyone connected. If there was a spine that maintained the structure of the family, it was her.

On Sunday evenings, he would usually reflect on the week that was and the week to come, and say silent prayers for God to keep everyone in the household safe.

The colors of the house were ocean blues, off whites, and grays with a splash of green here and there. Guests always commented that it was calm, serene, and inviting. It was a place to welcome family, friends, and other guests who were treated like family.

The man would frequently comment that he had his own live-in therapist since his wife had a doctorate in psychotherapy. As he had been a trial lawyer, a therapist in the house was both a good and, many times, a necessary thing.

In the early years of her career, the woman's practice mainly focused on survivors of childhood trauma. Soon she became an oracle. When a friend or family member needed help getting through a rough patch, the woman was the one they turned to. She was her husband's anchor during stormy weather and he didn't know where he would be without her.

The woman always said that her husband opened her up to adventure and she provided a safe harbor for him when calm was called for. They were the perfect match. Each truly completed the other.

The girls were nine and ten respectively when the family moved to Genesis Road. The couple chose the street name and number because the location represented a new beginning for the family. They so much wanted to slow things down and recapture that meaning of what life was meant to be. Yes, there would be work before they both stepped back from their careers, but maybe they could live here at a slower pace. The calm setting, the quiet moments, the support that they each needed to meet the potential of who and what they could each be—they were lucky that their respective careers provided them this chance.

Although he was not a religious man, the man who formerly lived at 1318 Genesis Road did believe in the idea that we are not alone in our journeys through life—that something more looks after us. Of the many religious and spiritual paths that he explored, he felt incredibly drawn to shamanism. He believed that there has to be a big, universal tale that embraces everyone. That our lives couldn't just be composed of individual moments unconnected one to the next and incidental encounters.

And the man believed that good intentions, decency, and honor were the core ingredients to a full and purposeful life. *If these qualities do not define a religious or spiritual person, then what would? Everything else,* he thought, *was mere ritual, decoration, and pomp.*

He also thought that if ritual, decoration, and pomp did not include good intentions, decency, and honor, the hypocrisy would stifle and strangle everyone involved in them, even so-called righteous people. Process should never overtake purpose. Ritual should never overshadow meaning. He often felt that people were more concerned with how they looked than with who they actually were, especially in the social media age.

When 1318 Genesis Road was being built, he felt that the dwelling place could make a statement on behalf of his whole family to whatever greater force or supernatural being was overseeing their lives, that they were creating an altar to the possibility of the "more" that was all around them. He hoped that this more would protect the family. He believed the house could even be a portal to the more.

In times of stress and strain, it is good to know we don't need to face our challenges alone, that we can connect to the greater story, the grander purpose, the beauty of the ever-expanding universe. Some people can only see small sections of life. They are distracted by the noise of the moment. If they would only step back, look up and out, and witness the miracle of each moment—the opportunity we have been given to participate in this experiment of living—they might be able then to breathe, relax, and enjoy their lives.

Life truly is a miracle.

The grander story of the couple and their daughters cannot be separated from their existence in the house on Genesis Road. The house became an integral part of the couple's existence. Like a member of the family. They greeted it when they entered, told it to be safe when they left for the day, and even said good night to it along with the rest of the family at bedtime.

For good luck, the man put up Tibetan prayer flags along the back fence behind the bridge that crossed the most-days-dry riverbed, right next to a large, concrete Buddha that watched over Genesis, his pet name for the house. Though he was not tied to any one religion or philosophy, he wanted to be part of the larger meaning of the journey of life on earth.

He also kept a Native American shaman's drum hanging under an eave on the back deck next to the fire pit. His thoughts about how to seek inner peace and keep an open heart were clearly eclectic. He always felt connected to the spiritual world. The infinite couldn't be captured in our finite temporal comings and goings. But what if it could? *What if we could connect to the infinite?* That question always intrigued him.

The man believed in multiple paths to the deeper meaning of a singular life. But he also believed there really is no such thing as an exceptional life because life itself is remarkable. He believed we can all experience being connected to each other and nature if we keep our egos in check; and that the idea of singularity is, in general, an ego motivation that separates people from each other.

He felt that if we just all took a breath we would all see the majesty of what is before us and there would be less animus between people.

The woman was more concrete in her thoughts about life, death, and the possibility of more. In her view, we are here and then not. She always would say that we should all try to make each day meaningful and live a life of purpose for once we are gone the story and journey is completed. That is why she always chose to be kind and giving. She felt this was her one time story and wanted it to be a gracious one.

Although the couple's philosophies were very different, they gave each other the space to explore their choices. To some extent, there was a thread that connected their views in that they chose goodness and decency as their touchstones.

The girls were still little when the house was finished. At the time the couple retired, it seemed just like yesterday when 1318 Genesis was designed and built, but it had already been over forty years. Over those years, it had its share of changing paint colors, wallpapers, furniture, flooring, carpeting, and tiles. The kitchen was redone four times and the bedrooms dozens, especially as the girls grew and went through their stages from baby to preteen to high schooler. They'd gone away to college and come back again to visit either alone or with friends or their latest love interests, then later, with their husbands and their own children.

Time is funny. Time can seem just to be there, standing in the corner, not bothering anyone; yet it is always moving, changing things, and affecting everything anywhere. Time is the constant endangered species in all our lives. Each moment vanishes once we've lived it, and it can never reappear. The tricky, most deceiving part of time is that because the moments keep coming (until they don't), we think that it is always going to be there. It is not.

Shock and sadness may hit us when this realization becomes concrete. But it is too late then to appreciate the gift of time that was so easily and cavalierly squandered.

Before the drywall went up, the man had walked around the house with a black magic marker and wrote on different beams: "God, protect this home and this family." And then, through forty years, Genesis stood there, protecting the man and his family and their precious moments in time. Whether it was quiet evenings alone when everyone else was away or Thanksgiving dinners when family and friends came from far and wide to fill the house with stories, memories, laughter, and tears, the house and its living room became a part of the history of the family. If the walls could talk, they would tell a never-ending tale of love, drama, comedy, tragedy, and romance, with some musical interludes.

He noticed that each house they visited had its own "feeling." That's why in some houses you can sense yourself feeling happy or anxious. Feeling any particular emotion. Scattered thoughts or sophisticated organization, loving emotions, or tension that you could not even cut with a knife. The house on Genesis Road seemed always to be humming. Upbeat. Hopeful. Full of possibility. Those feelings transferred from the family to the home and back again. They knew Genesis was there to protect them. It was a place to celebrate good times and to provide sanctuary to the family in tough times. They all felt safe once they were home and closed the front door.

Every family has its health challenges. Theirs were the usual bumps and bruises from minor car accidents and broken bones from sporting mishaps and slips in the bathroom. But as they aged, the man and woman had more major moments of need. He had open heart surgery and she had double hip replacement surgery. Through it all, Genesis patiently waited for the family to gather in the living room or on the back deck and comfort them while they recovered.

The man loved the house. In the quiet of some nights, he would thank the home for being there and protecting them all those years. He had always felt like a greater power was watching over the family, the house, and the very land it was built on. The woman felt the same way but attributed this to her feng shui efforts and the sweet, cozy environment she created using her design and gardening skills.

They did their best to repay the house in kind for how it was there for them. There were times when Genesis needed help and support: a roof leak here or there, a plumbing issue, even a few cracks in a wall or ceiling required tender loving care. They were there for Genesis.

On the kitchen wall by the refrigerator, you can still see the pencil lines of the height of the girls as they grew from year to year. For some reason, the redesigns never touched the all-important measuring corner by the refrigerator.

Particular locations in the house emanate positive energy. For instance, a wall by the back door exiting to the deck seems to vibrate at certain times of the day. You can feel warmth as you entered the house through the front door. The couple hung an OM symbol over the front door. They believed this made Genesis hum.

The man really never thought of it, but looking back on it later, he realized this was just the reality. There is a gentle embrace as you enter the house. It is as if the house sits on an energy vortex of some sort. He often wondered if the mountains in Montana where Genesis sits are an energy field, like the energy field in the Khumbu region of the Himalayas. That vortex is known for its eminently positive energy and providing moments of clarity and peace if you can slow down, breathe, and take in the majesty of the possible. He always wondered if Montana's vortex is an energy portal to the infinite.

Earth may be the one true deity that holds all the answers of life and death. Maybe it is this belief that attracted him to shamanism. Could there be a bridge to take them from birth to a rebirth? Maybe it was the same belief that attracted the woman to feng shui. Did the day come for them when these thoughts and even wishes could be realized? After all, earth offers us the water and food that sustain our lives, and cures for our ailments are contained in the various flowers, shrubs, and trees that grow in its soil. Could there be even more that earth can give us that we just can't believe is even possible . . . yet is?

The woman tended to the needs of Mother Earth—Gaia—in her garden and greenhouse. The man did the same by praying and drumming over the fields and streams in back of the house. Maybe appreciation for their efforts was coming due.

Could Gaia sense that the man and the woman were good people who did their very best year over year to honorably care for their patch of Gaia? Did Gaia notice the attention and care they gave her? Without fully understanding the significance of their location or their way of life, the couple sensed and responded to the energetic presence of the house on Genesis Road, which lay on a vortex that sits in the very heart of the infinite—and they were much loved. Could the quid pro quo be the truth in the unfolding journey of this family?

The house sits quiet now and waits for someone to return to occupy it. How could they have all left? Of course, the girls left long ago when they went off to college and then began their own lives and families. But now the man and his bride of over fifty years are gone too. A decision made during the isolation stage of the pandemic tests the limits of our faith. A choice that was irreversible.

Dust has settled on the tables and chairs. Spiders have set up house in the garage. An intimate online memorial service was held four months ago. For a while, the housekeeper, Claudia, would come in once a week to check on the house. She emptied the pantry and refrigerator months ago, and recently simply watered the plants and dusted the furniture. But the house felt so deserted without anyone residing in it that she resigned. Her absence has forced the daughters to come home. There are only faint echoes left from the times gone by when the family roamed the hallway. A realtor is now involved in preparing the property for a sale. The realtor has asked them to remove their possessions.

A massive oak tree stands in the backyard that has to be over fifty feet tall. When the girls were young, they climbed it. Their father hung a swing on one of its bigger branches. There was also a rope with a big Mack truck tire hanging off another branch. Oh, how the girls loved swinging from that tree. The tire and swing are silent and motionless.

Next to the tree is a wooden plaque reading:

"BLESS THE MAGIC OF THIS HOME.
FEEL THE POWER OF GENESIS."

The day their father bought that plaque, the girls were vacationing with their parents outside of Boone, North

Carolina, when they saw an old wood-carving shop. Their father asked the owner of the shop if he could create a plaque for their home in Montana. When they came back after lunch, a few hours later, the carver presented them with the plaque. It was perfect.

The house on Genesis Road had been their parents' home and sanctuary to the last breath. This was the spot where they lived, loved, and tried to come to terms with the meaning of their lives and how to overcome the obstacles to living well that face each of us. Every family has a story. There is always a beginning, then life plays out.

For them, much began with their arrival to Genesis Road and the wilds of Montana. But then, as in all things, there were endings. Sometimes endings will be followed by new beginnings. Life can surprise us that way. But for now, the house is, as if in hibernation, asleep to its future.

While the couple lived there, no matter what happened the day before, no matter what challenges faced the man or the woman or the whole family, they would get up in the morning and say to each other, "Good morning, my loves," and then say, "It is always beautiful in the morning." This was their way of saying: "We've got this: a new day, a new chapter, a new beginning." Genesis was a dynamic that underscored the way this one, small family lived.

Many people are locked into the yesterdays of their lives. Whether the man anticipated having a good day or a bad day, he wanted to believe that each morning was a rebirth, an unlocking from the chains of bad choices and events that occurred the day before.

Rebirths, they would all discover, comes in all shapes and sizes.

In the master bedroom closet, on the floor behind boxes of old tee shirts and sweatpants, an envelope lies. It is sealed and even has scotch tape over the seal to guarantee that the contents are safe. The envelope is business-sized and contains a letter of sorts, more than twenty pages long. Handwritten in blue ballpoint ink on the outside of the envelope are the words *REFLECTIONS AND RANDOM THOUGHTS.*

What is the letter doing in the closet? When was it written? Why was it written? Was it dropped there by accident, a set of personal notes that fell behind the clothes by mistake? Is it more diary than letter? Did the author of the letter intend for it to be found?

So many questions. All as yet unanswered. Maybe that is the way life is: Filled with hidden papers, secret corners, random thoughts, events in a life that no one knows about or is supposed to know about. So often he and his wife would talk about how sometimes they felt like they were a mystery to others and even themselves.

Does anyone really know the mind of another person— even a best friend, spouse, or parent?

The man spent a good deal of time in the last month of his life reflecting on whether he knew himself completely. There were many times when he had done or said things that seemed so out of character with who he thought he was. And he was fairly sure others did too. He wrote the letter for the sake of his daughters. The choice he and his wife were making to end their lives before she died of terminal causes was so out of character for them that he needed to make certain that it was explained not only to the girls, but also to himself. He knew they would eventually find the envelope when they were cleaning out the house on Genesis Road.

Whether its contents would be understood by them was something else.

2. Serendipity

It has been four months since the man and his wife made and acted upon their fateful decision. But events leading up to it began six months prior, when she was rushed by ambulance to the local hospital. Between those two time markers, his envelope landed behind the clothes in the master bedroom closet. Their decision evolved after the onset of the woman's illness.

The man had known his wife was not feeling well. At first, she covered it well. When she would speak with the girls she would just comment that she was feeling achy and then change the subject to talk about her beautiful grandchildren. Once he fully understood what was happening, he would simply tell the girls that their mom was under the weather. The girls had their own lives to lead, and what would it accomplish to worry them?

Despite his apparent nonchalance about the issue when he spoke with the girls, in his gut he just felt that this was going to be a serious illness. His wife had never complained about feeling sick until now.

Perhaps to calm himself, he felt the need to start writing about their love story and how they ended up living on

Genesis Road. He was proud of their relationship. The story deserved to be told of the triumphs and tragedies they experienced and of the love that filled the rooms and scented the air at Genesis Road. Their love affair was a marvel in a world of constant change. Their love was so deeply rooted that it had withstood the types of storms, upheavals, and intrusions that had vanquished the marriages of so many of their friends. Long ago, they had decided to weather the storms together. Once again, she was the glue and the spine that kept their life together humming, even when the disruptions would have shocked and destroyed lesser efforts and determination.

He had always heard it said that love is blind. As his wife's illness progressed, he came to understand this maxim better than he ever imagined he would. To him, this phrase meant seeing your love through the windows of your heart and soul, not merely through your eyes. Love is ageless and timeless because it exists outside the tangible world of tables, chairs, dishes, and cups.

Because love exists in the intangible world of dreams, desires, wishes, and romance, love does not register wrinkles and scars. If love sees them at all, it views them as signs of shared experiences either enjoyed or survived. Wrinkles and scars are badges of your shared journey. The bullets dodged, the cliff avoided, the death-defying twists to avoid a fate to which others may have succumbed.

He thought often about all they had been through together and his memories took on a life of their own. Memories are a time machine. It seemed to him that God must have created memories so that we can travel and relive moments on a dreamlike cruise through the years. By closing his eyes after looking at a still photograph, what happened before and after the snapshot was taken would come alive like a motion picture, and there he was in another time and place. Magical.

But now it is time to move past the memories and open up to the future.

As illness took hold of the woman, one night her husband sat down and began to write. He didn't know how her sickness was going to play out, so he wanted to memorize the details of the story of their life together. Would she survive? Would he survive if she didn't? The future was an unknown commodity.

The man was also casting about for insights on handling adversity. He wanted his daughters to be comforted in their grief at the loss of their parents when he wouldn't be able to guide them. In reflecting on the course of his life and how he himself had learned to persevere in the face of loss and when the going was rough emotionally, the man recognized that it was his spiritual beliefs that sustained him the most. He knew they'd be shocked by the news even if he tried to prepare them.

The woman's COVID came on fast, but it shouldn't have been unexpected. After all, there was a pandemic of the stuff. Like a raging, windblown brush fire on the dry, open prairie, it consumed everything in its path.

In the early days of COVID, it seemed like a hostile alien attacker from another planet. All it did was consume lives. First hundreds, then thousands. And then it killed millions around the world. The town, state, and country all went into lockdown. The world would never be the same. It affected all members of every family. Parents and children couldn't visit friends and other family members. Holidays became phone calls or zoom chats. Human connection became a thing of the past. Isolation brought all-new challenges and problems. The mental health of everyone was suffering. Life as it had been known became unknown in its new form. Normalcy was lost. A new normal was being created each day and it was unsettling.

Forced containment resulted in everyone turning inward. Fear gripped everyone. People need human contact. They need to be held, touched, hugged, caressed. Those emotional connections became lost notions of a bygone era. We weren't meant to live isolated from one another. The couple felt fortunate to have each other to share seclusion. There was a feeling of loneliness even though the phone and internet were available. Life became surreal. COVID seemed to sap the joy out of the days. The illness turned into a physical, emotional, and spiritual attack on everyone.

The unknown is scary. But when the unknown kills and there is no treatment, as it was at the beginning of the pandemic, the unknown simply becomes "the monster." It was a gigantic monster, King Kong and Godzilla wrapped in one big, ugly bundle. The world turned inward. People started washing the outside of every bag and box that was either delivered by the grocery store or dropped off by a friend. No one went out to the corner store or pharmacy. Doctors' consultations were by phone. In-person moments of contact were few and far between. Family and friends couldn't even get to physically say their goodbyes in the last moments of a life. At best goodbye was said on the phone or in a Zoom chatroom. It was heartbreaking.

And COVID turned the afflicted into something resembling Jeff Goldblum's *The Fly* creation. Morphing from healthy to having no ability to smell or taste, fever, chills, the sweats, congested lungs, blood clots circulating throughout the body, and more were common stories covered by the news media. The hospitals filled up fast. Ambulance sirens drowned out any other sound day and night. Portable morgues were becoming common in the major cities. Death for a time became as commonplace as the air we breathed.

Even the air itself began to take on the features of an enemy. Breathing depended on where you were and to whom you were close. First stay four feet apart, then maintain a distance of six feet became the advice. The norm. Masks became a fashion accessory. Washing hands over and over again was felt to be mandatory. Staying two yards away from everyone felt so strange that you began to feel you were living in a dystopian society.

To a great extent, the world was an unknown setting. It felt as if it had stopped. And in many ways it did. Airports were empty. Trains and buses were believed dangerous to ride. Designating seating was established everywhere. There was a sense that a metamorphosis was occurring, but lacked a clear vision of the new shape the world would take. It was hard to trust that all would one day be well again. They believed that things would never again be the same. People seemed to change. Frustration, anger, hostility, and fear of the unknown were unleashed everywhere you looked. Businesses shut down, stores closed, theaters were empty, restaurants became obsolete. World economies were shaking.

And then, COVID hit the house on Genesis Road.

The woman had a preexisting condition with her kidneys, so she was at risk. She caught it. It started with a cough. Then she got chills. Then came cold sweats and fever. Then she was feeling weaker and just plain awful and scared. She lost her appetite and started losing weight. She was always the brave one, yet he could see the fear in her eyes.

They talked about letting the girls know of her severe illness, but were trying to figure the best way. How to explain the potential loss of the one in the family who kept the rhythm flowing so effortlessly? The couple finally decided to set up a FaceTime chat with the girls. Even though they both felt that parents should care for and worry about their children and not the other way around, they made the call to Sarah and Rachel. They filled the girls in on what was going on. They both got on the call and told them that their mom was feeling awful because she had a bad case of COVID, but that they were hopeful. Their mom told them not to worry. That was just her nature.

Both girls were terribly upset and frustrated. They were trying to balance their desire to be there for their mom against their worries about protecting their immediate families, especially their children, from this horrid virus.

Their mom told them that she loved them so, and no matter what happened she would always be there for them, one way or another. The girls didn't want to hear that kind of talk and said that life without her would be simply unbearable. She tried to comfort them. Their dad said they would set up regular calls to keep them updated.

Sarah and Rachel told their parents they longed to be at Genesis with them both but this damnable disease was the ultimate barrier to human touch. They each gave the other long looks and virtual hugs and then the girls, almost in unison, said, "We love you, Mommy."

The man never mentioned what he was considering. He thought it would be just too much for them to handle. Also, he was a bit fearful that if he decided to do what he was contemplating they might try to intervene to prevent it.

The man set up the second bedroom for himself so that his beloved wife could have the bigger room with the bathroom right next to her. This went on for a week or two, but then her condition just became too severe. She was having a hard time breathing. At that point, he called 911 and an ambulance took her to the hospital.

Frankly, they anguished over that decision because in the age of COVID once a patient was in the hospital no visitors were permitted. Besides, the doctors didn't have an answer yet to the question of treatment. The health industry was making it up as they went along.

Furthermore, being away from his wife for any length of time was always difficult for the man. Life without her seemed empty and cold.

He told the girls that their mom was in the hospital. The girls knew what that meant. They knew they couldn't visit her even if they wanted to. The anguish for everyone was unbearable. The girls told their dad that they each were going to create a video that they would send to him to see if he can get it to a nurse in the hospital to play for her. They did that. These were messages of love and devotion. Their husbands and children made appearance on the video to tell stories, share memories and send kisses and prayers of getting better.

The man was foolishly hopeful, but everything changed when his wife took the turn for the very worst. He then went into survival mode. It was when someone at the hospital phoned to explain they wanted to intubate her that he realized this was probably not going to end well.

Early in the pandemic, the doctors stuck with the intubation protocol. Later, studies started to show that this might not be the best way to go. He panicked when he heard that they wanted to intubate and decided Genesis was calling. He realized that he had to call the girls and prepare them for the worst possibility. But first he wanted to meet with the doctor.

He finally was able to speak to the doctor and was told that his wife was not doing well. "You should prepare your family," he was told. In response, he said he wanted to take her home. The doctor argued with him. He got on the phone with her and explained everything to her. She agreed that she wanted to be at Genesis. She felt that the warmth, balance, beauty, and energy of Genesis was calling her. She wanted to be by her garden and see all her beautiful butterflies.

And one comment she made captured his attention. She said she thought Genesis would heal her. His memory started to emit flashes of guardians and guides he'd met during a long ago shamanic journey he had taken. But these were just flashes. It was a beautiful idea.

She wanted to speak with Rachel and Sarah, to see them one more time, she told him. The comment was shocking to his system. The final admission of her impending death. He didn't answer, but simply nodded. He knew he had to provide them all with the moments to share stories and say their goodbyes. He said once he got her home he would set up the call.

So, the man signed all the release papers and absolved the hospital of any liability. She was looking forward to getting to Genesis.

She looked at him as they got back to Genesis and said that there is such limited time left and she was glad they were home. She wanted to sit on the deck and look at the dry riverbed, the trees, the bridge, her flowers. She wanted to see life in all its colors and movements. Their home was her sanctuary. Whether looking out over the field and forest on the ridge or sitting by the fireplace in the living room, it sure beat the confines of a dimly lit hospital room.

All he could think about was her and his love for her.

As she sat on the deck covered by blankets and looking out over the mountain range, they called the girls. It was the saddest, sweetest, most painful conversation he ever heard and yet it was also beautiful. Love is magical. He left the three of them to their conversation. He went into the den. It was over an hour before he heard her call for him. She said that a good part of the time with the girls were them all just looking at each other. Staring into each other's eyes. So much of communication is nonverbal. The mindful gaze. They all acknowledged the delicate moment in time and the gratitude they felt for each other.

"Thank you, Mommy."

"Thank you, my sweet babies."

For most people, the death of a beloved spouse or family member is a terrifying horror movie; and you can't walk out of the theater.

The clothes are still there. The shoes. The smells. The makeup. The prescription pill containers. Menus from favorite restaurants. Everything that is part of a life, but not the life itself. Pictures. Inscriptions on sticky notes that are reminders of things to do, like get the car serviced, go to doctor appointments, do shopping. We all keep to-do lists. Everyone has routines. These are parts of the story of a life.

The man was always told that death is the final curtain call. *But what if that is just not the case at all?* he mused. *What if death finally provides us with that stimulation to break away from the small story of a life and become connected to the grander story of infinite possibilities?* He used to say that we are finite beings existing in an infinite universe and yet we think it all begins and ends with our physical presence here. That just seemed so narrow a way to see existence.

He thought about what he had seen typically happen to a mourner's memory after a loved one dies. There are turning point moments when the bad times seem to evaporate. The good times are exaggerated. Then, you only remember the laughter. The parties. The love making. The baby's first steps. The glass of wine before a quiet dinner just for two. The look in the eyes. The smiles. The touch. The tender caress.

But what if instead of reliving personal experiences, we allowed our loved one's "death" to open up an energy field in which we ourselves could witness their transition from the body into the spirit world and then become one with the majesty and magic of a realm or dimension of being of the like that only science fiction and fantasy filmmakers have created on screen? *What if it is possible to see beyond our five senses and enter a state where we are pure energy and at one with the infinite universe?* What if we never really leave?

He thought about how the five senses cannot capture all the possibilities and potential of life. The sixth sense, for him, was a force more than the sum of our parts. *What if this becomes the new reality when we are rid of our earthly bodies?*

Even as his wife was fading from this moment in time, he himself was undergoing a metamorphosis of sorts. A transformation. He began to see the house on Genesis Road as a form of a cocoon. *Can a human "caterpillar" transform into a spiritual "butterfly"? Is it possible to ascend to the next level of being and bypass disease or injury?* He liked to contemplate the possibility that he could learn how so that he never had to be separated from his bride.

Some days he felt despondent, not just for himself but for the whole world. We have messed it all up so royally. He thought that it would just be so disappointing and demoralizing to think we are here for just a blink of a cosmic eye and do so much damage to our planetary home. It comforted him to imagine that this life is only a small wrinkle in the fabric of a greater reality.

Is there, in truth, a bigger, more profound kind of life awaiting all of us? Is this merely some sort of preamble to that tale—a preliminary side show? After all, we are on a small planet in an ocean of time and space that science tells us keeps expanding. It seemed egotistical to him to assume that being human is that important, that we are the end game of the universe, that we are the "it" and it begins and ends for us. *It just can't be so.*

Maybe the impact of the life-threatening illness of his love brought him to recognize the inherent truth that life is more than we ever imagined—though we have forgotten what our ancestors knew about how to tap into that which is *more.* In his travels, he had encountered many people who described strange and marvelous phenomena and guided him to sample them as best he could. But he felt different now, readier than ever to learn. Maybe these dire conditions were an opportunity to be released from the humdrum regimen of trying merely to survive from one moment to the next.

He began to view the challenge of his wife's impending death as a spiritual opportunity. *It could be a transform-ation and transition period for us both if we open our hearts and souls at the same moment to the universal "story."* There was more to come—in his heart he was certain—and he wanted them to experience it together. But there was work to be done.

He was truly terrified. What if he was wrong and this was all there was to be for any of us. If that was so then he was making colossal bad choices and decisions. Maybe he had to get her back to the hospital. His mind was swirling but then he stopped himself and centered himself in Genesis. The energy. The power. The grandeur. They were not going to act out of fear. They were going to journey beyond fear. The magical unknown awaited them both.

He decided to write a letter to explain his actions to Rachel and Sarah, and also to tell them about six strangers he had met by serendipity over the span of decades that affected his life for the better. These six strangers opened a door for him to have faith in a mystical realm and shifted the direction of his life—and theirs by extension. He hoped that the lessons these individuals taught him would help his daughters navigate their own challenges.

Sometimes a serendipitous meeting between strangers has a greater impact on a life than any planned engagement with an old friend. He felt sure that the strangers didn't know the impact they were having on him. In *Tao Te Ching* it is written: "When the student is ready, the teacher appears." He guessed he had been ready to learn something from these "teachers." Each shared or demonstrated a thought, an observation, a positive attitude, or a way out of a negative or challenging moment. Life had brought them both to this moment to show them all the way. Life can surprise us that way.

He looked down at the pen in his hand. He pulled the paper closer to the edge of the desk. Maybe these ideas would register with them, and help them through the sorrow and anguish they are feeling at this point in their lives. He also wanted to give them a glimpse of his ideas about spiritual metamorphosis. Whether or not they would think him insane for believing what he did about transitioning out of his physical body simultaneously with his wife, he wanted to comfort them and explain as best he could what had transpired at the end.

His mind flashed to his girls. Sarah. Rachel. Sweetness multiplied. They were the light of his life. They had grown up to be accomplished in different ways, and both were bright and wise beyond their years. Gentle, kind people. He was so proud of them.

Sarah was the oldest. She was married and had a son who was now in college. Rachel was "the baby." They always called her that no matter her age. She was also married. Her daughter was getting ready to apply to colleges. Watching their baby have a baby had been mindblowing.

Becoming a grandparent was exciting and had made him reflect on how fast time passes. He would always shake his head when he thought about his kids having kids. Seemed impossible that time had gone by so fast.

People transform. He and his wife went from being kids to being lovers to husband and wife, and then to being parents to grandparents. This was part of their process of metamorphosis. He could see and feel the transformations happening to him, and to all those whom he brought into the world and their families.

The girls and their families lived far away from Genesis Road. Sarah lived in Portland, Oregon. She'd gone to the University of Oregon, where she studied psychology, and now had a thriving private practice specializing in child psychology and the treatment of trauma.

Rachel lived even further afield in London, England. While attending the University of Southern California, she'd studied abroad one summer at the University of Westminster in England, one of the finest art schools there are. She fell in love with photography, stayed overseas, and in time became known as one of the finest commercial photographers in London. Diverse companies hired her for advertising campaigns and image branding.

He decided that after he wrote this letter he would seal it. He wasn't certain what he was going to do yet, but that didn't matter right now. The writing was cathartic. He needed to go deep inside to find some peace.

He wrote about the house on Genesis Road and the energy vortices he believed existed in the land it stood upon. He wrote down his thoughts and feelings about his memories of the early years of their family. He didn't want to forget the exquisite moments that shifted his life for the better. He wanted to experience them all again and remind the girls of what treasures they were to him and their mother. Then he wrote about his philosophy and those who had impacted him. He wondered if it would seem as relevant and meaningful to his children as it was to him.

When he was done, he left it on a ledge in the master closet. How it subsequently fell onto the floor where he use to drop some tee shirts before he put them in the washer he didn't see or know.

So many events then occurred and choices kicked into play that he soon forgot about the letter. The trauma of the impending loss of his love of over fifty years turned him inward. It made him very quiet and introspective and focused him on the meaning of a life. He had to come to terms with it. He was slowly coming to terms with the choice and the meaning of Genesis in their life.

Claudia found the couple's bodies. She had cleaned and tidied up the house on Genesis Road for over fifteen years. Every Monday she was there bright and early. She had a key to the house. After ringing the doorbell and knocking, she entered and called out their names. She was confused that there was no answer since their car was in the driveway and there wasn't another there for an overnight health aide. That meant they must be home. She knew about the mortal illness, the hospital stay, and hospice. But no one was answering, so she walked into the bedroom.

That's where Claudia found them both. They were lying on the bed in white robes holding hands and seemed just to be serenely sleeping. They had their eyes closed and it seemed to Claudia that they each had a smile on their face. They looked at peace.

Claudia didn't touch anything. She called the couple's daughters right away to tell them what she'd found and express her sorrow. They told her to call 911. Claudia said, "Maybe their deaths has something to do with COVID." Sarah and Rachel were puzzled. They knew their mom had been ill, but their dad?

Claudia waited for the police and paramedics to arrive. She gave a statement, then went home leaving everything in the house as it was. Sarah and Rachel said they would fly to Montana immediately to handle the arrangements for their parents' physical remains.

After they hung up with the housekeeper, the women called all the different phone numbers they had for their parents' friends and extended family . . . nieces, nephews, aunts, uncles, and cousins. They kept reaching out to other family members and friends far and wide. Everyone was surprised, saddened, and confused.

Still in shock but buoyed by the need to be pragmatic, Sarah contacted her parent's lawyer, a woman who had drafted all their legal documents from wills to trusts and deeds.

The lawyer said that she was not aware of anything being at all different lately. She told them she would review everything and contact the accountant and stock advisors to see if they knew anything about the couple's condition at the end of life. She asked if it was okay for her to go to the house to make certain all was well or to wait.

Sarah said to wait. She and Rachel would arrive the next day to investigate themselves.

Their parents' mutual passing was truly a mystery.

3. A Love Story

How to explain a love that is unending? Not some storybook romance but one that has been tested by time, circumstance, hardship, bad judgment, forgiveness, and a passion that goes beyond the physical and enters the world of the mystical? The desire of the partners always to be with each other? Their passion to live within the aura of the other?

The chief characteristic of the couple's love was that it always seemed to be fresh. New. The husband felt excited to wake up next to his wife each morning. He felt lucky. He believed she made him a better person. A better man. When she went away, either to visit the kids or to spend time with her close friends, he was happy for her, but felt a little lost and lonely.

It may sound odd. He was not despondent. Not sad. He just had an empty type of feeling.

When his wife was out of town, he would fill the time with reading and writing and music. He loved old songs. Of course, as he got older, "old songs" moved from being produced in the Forties and Fifties to the Sixties, Seventies, and Eighties. Even a few songs from the Nineties snuck into his playlist, but songs written after that just didn't connect with him. For him, what mattered in a song was that it touched a memory, a dream, a hope, or a tender human quality. "It's Impossible" by Perry Como still made him pause wherever he was when he heard it and smile and nod to himself.

He really didn't believe his daughters had thought much about their parents' love for each other. What adult children do? Most people find navigating the details of their own day takes all their focus. His daughters had husbands and children of their own, and professional obligations. He didn't fault them for focusing on those important elements in their lives. They saw each other several times a year during holiday seasons. However, the girls' busyness meant that when either he or his wife got ill, the two of them just took care of the other. They each became good nurses.

The decades flew by from the time they met, dated, fell in love, and journeyed from day to day, year to year, adventure to adventure, and misadventure to misadventure, developing an understanding and appreciation for each other's qualities. There is a knowing that comes with the passage of time. They knew each other. And they really liked each other.

He frequently told his beloved that they would be together no matter what. He would look directly into her eyes and say, "Our souls are tied together as one."

She would smile, and being the more pragmatic one of the two, reply, "Oh honey, that's sweet. It's such a nice thought. But you were always the one thinking there was another journey after this one. I am not so sure."

"Just wait and see," he would say mysteriously. "I know things. Remember I once traveled to the other side with a shaman in Peru."

Then they would laugh.

This became a little ritual for them as they got older. But they hadn't taken it too seriously until now. By the time the illness was making a strong stand, they both recognized that it was never going to release her. The prospect of living without her was devastating to the man.

The house on Genesis Road was turned into a mini-hospital wing. The couple rented a hospital bed with railings on both sides that moved up and down when you pressed a button. The nightstand by the bed became its own drugstore. Bed pans, tissues, different medications, and cold compresses were everywhere, so whatever was needed was always in easy reach. They also hired a nurse who would come in around dinner time and spend the night. His wife wanted him to get some rest, and he wanted to make certain she had all she needed in case her symptoms worsened overnight. Nighttime always haunted him. The night seemed to get longer due to sickness and fear. In the darkness, demons would come to visit and pollute his mind with awful thoughts and nightmares.

Her condition was getting worse. She was deteriorating. It was more of a watch-and-wait situation than a situation including an expectation—or hope—of recovery. She had wonderful, lucid moments. But there were more moments in which she was either entirely quiet or tossing, moaning, and coughing. Both types of sleep were frightening. Her fever would spike, then subside following medication.

While she was lucid and reasonably awake, he would pull a chair next to her bed, hold her hand, and they would talk. Not about the now but about their past adventures and memories of uncontrolled joy and laughter. Like the time when they bought Sarah her first bicycle and she literally levitated in joy at seeing it being wheeled down the aisle in the toy store toward the cashier. Or the time that Rachel first stepped onto the sand at the beach, plopped herself down, looked up, and could not stop giggling. At two and a half, Rachel thought sand was the greatest invention of all time. The lucid moments would last for maybe a few minutes every few hours during the daytime hours and then fade to a silence, a stare, a longing, a quiet anguish that he could sense and feel deep in his soul around dusk.

The doctors convinced the couple that the woman should take some sedatives in the evening to help her get through the night. The thought was that perhaps if she slept through the night, she would have more strength during the day. Sometimes this worked. More often than not, it didn't. But they nonetheless kept that regimen going.

Most of the time, the man sat beside his wife and watched her, held her hand, put a cool wet cloth on her forehead, and told stories about their shared memories. "Do you remember that trip, that adventure, that restaurant, that birthday celebration when . . . ?" He would also read to her. She had loved her spy and murder mysteries with iconic detectives, so he would read parts of these types of books to her throughout the day. His intention was to keep life lighter than it was. Time seemed to slow down, especially during the tough moments. Episodes of difficulty breathing and coughing spells were becoming more frequent.

Time was a critical presence in their lives. It seemed that the only thing of relevance was the passage of time.

During the daylight hours, the man made sure the blinds were up so the sunlight came into the room. The master bedroom was an east-facing room, so mornings typically were bright and welcoming. The room filled with sunbeams, and his wife felt their warmth on her face. When she turned her head directly toward the sun, she looked like a little girl reaching for an unreachable treasure. He would stare at the individual sunbeams as they entered the room. They caught some dust in the air, and, it seemed to him, even took on different colors as they made their way to her face.

There were occasional moments when a prism of light filled the room. Noticing this, at one point she started slightly humming "Somewhere Over the Rainbow." He felt like that moment was the fulfillment of a dream she'd once had, a sign of a beautiful destiny that was unfolding.

Being forever a poet and philosopher, he amused himself by wondering, *Will she wake up in another time and place when she dies? Is there another time and place she* could *wake up in—somewhere over the rainbow, past the pain, sorrow, and fear of our world? The mystics talk of such things.* Like a Make-a-Wish for a grownup.

As he pondered whether it was possible to choose to leave the body before dying, he would go out to the back deck. There he would wander near to the prayer flags so he could listen to them snap in the wind. His mind would go revisit memories of mystical experiences as he banged on his drum. He also would sit next to the Buddha statue in the yard some days and simply ask for help.

Time and life are such puzzles. They hardly make sense. You work. You strive. You love. You marry. You have children. And on and on. But to what end? What's the objective? Sooner or later, if you have a life partner, one of you will find yourself sitting at the bedside of the one who means the most to you as they take their last breath. In that quiet moment, all you can do is be present. Probably more present than ever before because you know there is no other place you would rather be. No other place to go to. Nothing more important. Finally.

No multitasking should be done at that point. Better to be single-minded. Focused like never before. Put all your focus on your partner's life. The life that is not yours.

The question rushing through the man's mind now was, *Are there truly only relationships—not individual lives? Are we human if we don't have a way of connecting not just with other people, but with animals, plants, the mountains, the streams, and oceans—and the universe itself?* He longed to be connected to the cosmos!

If energy is our common denominator, then we cannot be truly alive unless we are connected to a larger, grander story. A story of biblical proportions. A story that began before we physically appeared. A story that continues after our bodies dissolve.

If this were not the case, then we would be nothing more than empty plastic containers bobbing in the middle of a vast ocean. The man couldn't believe that this would be our destiny. All this majesty put in place for just a fleeting second in the history of time and space. *We can't just be here having no lasting value, meaning, direction, intention, or reason.*

The man went into the den and sat down at his desk, then moved over to his easy recliner chair, took out more paper and his pen. He was writing by hand, not typing on a computer. A computer-generated note would come across as too impersonal at a highly personal time in all their lives. Besides, he wanted the girls to feel the words, not just read the words. When you handwrite there is part of you on the paper.

The den was quiet. It was on the west corner of the house, so it was not the brightest room in the house. That was until the late afternoon when the sunset would sneak through the half-drawn curtains and light the room up in a still life painting kind of way. Then the room would become a study in shades.

As he looked out the window, he could see the snow-covered mountains. Snow-covered, even in May. That was just the way Montana was at that time of year. He heard thunder in the distance. Rolling thunder. It was as if God wanted to be heard at that exact moment. He could sense God's presence. It was as if God entered the den and was hovering over him. He was no longer alone.

He picked up the pen. He wanted his beautiful daughters to know more about what he and their mom thought about things. Sarah and Rachel believed they knew their parents well. But he knew there were some stories they'd never heard before. It was the right time to tell them about the six people he met who informed his spiritual beliefs and confirmed to him that the decision he was considering implementing was the right decision.

This would be the last letter he ever wrote. He began:

"My dearest Sarah, Rachel,

"By this time, my darlings, you know that your mom and I are gone. I am so sorry for not telling you the whole story ahead of time. I probably handled this very badly and I hope you find it in your hearts to forgive me and try to understand the choices made. Our love for you is undying and forever. I hope this will soothe some of your pain and even give you a glimpse into a world that might be new to you both.

Our topic today is metamorphosis. As you know your mother is sick with COVID and the severity of her illness has me ruminating. There are things I would like you to know—lessons I learned that I want to hand down. The first of these is that we are always transitioning and have been given the gift of creating ourselves and the world we choose to live in. Change is part of our nature. Even before birth we are morphing from one form to another. After birth that truth continues. And it never ends. Please view our passing as a natural transition.

"I always wanted to be part of something more. Yet throughout my early years, I never felt that way. I always felt isolated and alone . . . even in a crowd. I felt like the odd one out. The one not chosen when the teams were being picked for any sport or game. The small one who couldn't block the basketball shot or swing the bat with enough force to get past the infield. There was never any encouragement to be more, so I didn't stretch myself.

"This feeling lasted all through elementary school and into junior high school. The acne on my face and my slim build did not help. It was only in ninth grade that I began exploring how I defined myself. I began to feel changes. I was too young to connect the dots, so to speak, so I did not understand that we are always changing. How we are always transitioning. It never stops.

"Some people see life as simply getting older and eventually losing our youthful glow, then disintegrating. But I see the process of living and aging as a much deeper and more meaningful aspect of a cosmic experiment. Change is not a negative. The change of aging make you ready for even greater changes to come.

"Life in a body is a warmup to the real adventure. It is an opportunity for the discovery of your unique gifts and talents. What some might criticize as a flaw

or shortcoming may actually be the very thing that triggers your unique talent or gift.

"For me, it had to do with a book I picked up at a used book shop I passed while walking home from the local convenience candy store one day. The used bookstore was always a fun place to wander. It was a bit dusty and many of the books were stained and really worn, yet it was a great place to scavenger-hunt for odd or left-behind tales. I have always loved authors and artists who tried and tried but never broke through. Sometimes an artist just has to be at the right place at the right time. The right person has to read the book and want to assist. But that doesn't happen too often. Sometimes just pure unvarnished luck is required.

"Finding a hidden treasure by an unknown talent is so rewarding. How many gems are never discovered because the seekers in a store either went for a more conventional choice or the cobwebs were too off-putting to scrape away so they never uncovered the writer's gift? There are probably answers to the greatest riddles of life lying lonely and unread everywhere. I almost want to run around yelling like a town crier to ensure that these writers and artists didn't waste their time and talent. They helped someone.

"Don't be discouraged. How many great thoughts or helpful hints that could help so many people are never discovered. We don't give ourselves the opportunity to find the answer to some long, lingering question when we ignore the book or thoughts in some magazine that is just one shelf away from the flavor-of-the-month crowd pleaser.

"Sarah, Rachel, seek out the author, book, artist that you find of interest even if the 'in crowd' and

'influencers' ignore them. You might just find a 'flashlight' that will lead you out of a dark moment. What others overlook might just be your long-sought answer to a troubling question.

"Reading has helped me through the years. And it started with this most unlikely book. It was sticking up from a pile of sports books. Normally I would have skipped it, but I saw the word kid *and pulled it out from the five books on top of it.*

"The book, The Kid Who Batted 1.000, *was written by Bob Allison and Frank Ernest Hill. It told the fanciful story of an improbable baseball season for one kid who made a difference with his unique, unexpected gift. This one talent changed the season for the whole team. I won't tell you what the gift was, since it doesn't matter to its impact on me, but if you are interested you can still find the book online, I think.*

"Anyway, some would say that the kid didn't have a talent at all. But they would be proven to be wrong. I figured that we each have such a gift, but we need to discover it and not be afraid to express it.

"I once heard it said that you can't complain unless you at least take the bat in your hands, step up to the plate, and swing. It helped me move outside my own fears and perceived limitations. I stopped listening to the naysayers who said I was too small or too this or that.

"As I said before, don't give up. You each have a unique gift and you will embrace it. I see it now as you have grown into the amazing women you have become. I realized that . . . "

He heard some noise from the bedroom.

The man jumped up from his recliner when he heard his wife call his name. He rushed into the bedroom to find her standing beside the nightstand. She was sweating and he could tell she was cold. Her hands were shaking. Shivering was more like it. All she had on was her black pajamas. He grabbed the blanket and wrapped it around her shoulders. She leaned into him. Her head nestled on his shoulder. She lifted her right arm and touched his face. There were tears rolling down her face and her nose was running.

He wiped her nose with his hand and then wiped his hand on his pant leg. He held her tight. She seemed to have lost more weight and looked so frail. She was a combination of a little girl and a tired prize fighter who just finished the twelfth round of a championship match.

To him she was both of those . . . a little girl and a defending champion boxer. She never ceased to amaze him. He never knew where all her strength came from. But she was always ready to get on with the task at hand. It didn't matter if it were after a long tough day or in the middle of a storm, she would simply say that the job of the day had to get done and who else was going to do it. She would and always did get it done. No complaints. No frowns. No afterthoughts.

And this moment was no different.

She looked up at him and said, "Did you pick the girls up from school yet? I don't want them getting wet in this rainstorm. Are they home already? Did they eat yet? Are they okay? How was school today? Do they have homework? You know Sarah needs help with her math and Rachel needs help in her spelling. Let me see them. I want to see them."

He pulled her close to him. He said they were both fine, they had eaten dinner, and he'd helped them do their homework. He said they were playing now, and he would bring them in to kiss her good night before bedtime. This seemed to calm her down.

She asked if he would help her get back into bed. She was weary and wanted to close her eyes just for a moment.

He got her back in bed, kissed her on her forehead, and told her he would bring some water for her to sip. She smiled that little girl smile and closed her eyes.

He realized that they were both entering a new place. A place neither had been before. A place neither wanted to be.

Why he didn't get COVID, he never understood. It was one of the anomalies of this particular virus. Some caught it. Some didn't. On exposure, some got a slight case, others none at all. And some fell under its grip, and it didn't let go. Was it the immune system? Preexisting conditions? Blood type? Or just the way fate plays out?

Life plays out the way it plays out with no reason behind it so often. We cannot prepare for all its sudden twists and turns.

They had reached a place in life where the path gets steeper. The steps are no longer evenly separated; nor are they smooth and sturdy enough to walk upon. The gravel is loosened and, if you are not careful, your foot slips on the climb, whether upward or downward. Here the steps were misshapen cobblestones. He knew where the path led; he just didn't know how long a walk they were in for. He only prayed it would be a peaceful walk and that a moment of clarity would arrive when he could say what had to be said and give thanks for her sharing her life with him.

At this moment he felt good that the girls and their mom had been talking and had said the things they needed to say to each other. They thanked each other for sharing their lives with each other. The three women had a bond that even death couldn't break.

As he was delivering the water to his wife's bedside, he kept thinking about metamorphosis. Transitions. Transformations. Maybe the place they had arrived did not have to be the end of their time together but rather could become a new beginning. A new beginning for all of them.

He went back to the den to continue his letter. He felt compelled to provide some fatherly advice. He began to feel as if the letter was turning into an anthem of sorts. A choral composition for his girls that they could reread at intervals to help them along the way. A spiritual guide to overcome obstacles and bypass bad people.

He continued:

"Sarah, Rachel, I want you to accept yourselves just as you are. That will liberate you from criticism, self-doubt, and the feeling of never being enough. Learn to embrace yourself flaws and all. If I'd accepted that I was a flawed human being earlier in my life, it would have opened up so many more possibilities for me and permitted me to lighten up and not take everything so damned seriously.

"It's easy to think the world revolves around us. It doesn't. We are so hard on ourselves. Don't take everything personally. Try not to fight the current so much. Find the way to tell your story without swimming upstream and always remember that"

The phone rang breaking his stream of consciousness. He looked at the number and the ID. It was the doctor's office. He hesitantly reached for the phone. He felt it was not going to be anything good. The nurse said to please wait, and the doctor would get right on.

The doctor then said that, with his wife's preexisting conditions, and due to the fact that she was not in the hospital, he felt this was truly just an assisted suicide and he was conflicted on how best to address this situation. The doctor reminded the man that his responsibility was to try to preserve life and not be part of a concerted effort to end a life. The doctor also said that he was not a spiritual advisor but a healer. He hinted at his concern that he should perhaps call the authorities.

The man told the doctor that he wanted to honor his wife's wishes. This was not a suicide. She was trying to eat and drink water, and was resting. She had a right to choose how to live her life even though she was gravely ill. Choices are made. There are consequences.

He then said, "Please let her and us be. . . . please. Look doctor, I love my wife. I would do anything for her. She simply wants to recuperate at home." He hoped that his request would give the doctor enough comfort to let it go. And what he said was the truth. Of course, he did not talk about the choices he was thinking about for himself.

The doctor said he understood and was available if they needed anything during the woman's "recovery" period. The man smiled hearing that last comment.

They said goodbye and the man hung up, then he headed back into the bedroom.

He sat on the edge of the bed. His wife was sleeping. He looked at her and only saw sweetness.

When they first met, they fell in love almost instantly. He immediately saw her kindness. Although she was gentle, she liked a challenge—and this meant she felt he was worth the effort. She saw a spirit of adventure in him that she also had in her which would take them on adventures across the world. With him, there was the potential to experience sights, sounds, and flavors of faraway cultures, and encounter people who would become their good friends and enrich their lives.

She opened her eyes and asked him what he was doing. He said, "Looking at you."

She said, "I look a mess."

"No, you do not!" he said emphatically. "You are as beautiful as the day we met."

"Liar," she said, then smiled and requested, "Tell me a story. Any story . . . just make it happy."

He looked down at his folded hands, looked up and began.

"There was a time, not long ago, when love mattered. A time when kindness was the currency of the land. There was a place where the sun was bright, and the sky was clear. At night you could see the moon and stars as clearly as never before because there was no ever before—this was the beginning of it all.

"It was Genesis. It was green and blue, and primary colors filled the senses. It was a time before the polluters and the thieves arrived. There were some small animals around, but they stayed to themselves.

"It was a time and place where magic was possible.

"God was everywhere and in everything. There was no divisions or divisiveness . There was no duality. There was just the whole. And in that setting, there were two children . . . just me and you, my love."

Her eyes met his. She whispered, "Can we go back there?"

"Yes."

"When"

"Soon."

"My love . . . we will go back there together. I promise." A flicker of a memory shot across his mind. Peru. *Yes, of course . . . Peru!*

He realized at that exact moment that there was a way. It was possible. It had to be. They could go "there" together. If what he had learned years before was true, they could cross over together and they could even communicate with Rachel and Sarah!

She closed her eyes and fell right to sleep. He walked back to the den to write.

The house was again quiet. He didn't want to wake his wife, so he decided to put his headphones on and listen to the music of Ana Vidovic. Her guitar playing was magical. It transported him to a spiritual place within himself.

As the music filled his soul, a path seemed possible. He knew what he had to do. The solution was there all along, he had just forgotten it. He hoped he had enough time to relearn the lesson he'd been taught. He hoped his wife's journey would wait a bit longer for him to prepare, but he knew he had no control over this deadly virus.

He picked up where he left off with his letter. But now he was writing both to his daughters and for himself to help him recall the way to make the crossing over and form of rebirth possible.

"Always remember, there are living, human guardians around you. You can call on them to guide you, help you, and give you comfort. These people may not be immediately obvious to you. They might appear in different forms than you expect. Trust your instincts, intuition, and open up to the kind stranger who suddenly enters your life, as they may be a guardian.

"Girls, for me, there were six guardians who appeared as strangers and changed my life for the better; and because of this, they changed our family's

life for the better. I will tell you about the first one now, as I might rely on his teachings again to help your mom and me to journey to a new, unexplored destination. He was an Indigenous elder I encountered in Peru.

"Before I tell you about this shaman, and the rest of my guardians, I will let you know right up front that the lesson I hope you take from this is to be open to new people and the possibilities of life. So much of life is just luck . . . being at the right place at the right time, and saying yes to an invitation or connection. Live with your arms open, not folded inward. Life has a way of beating a person down. It doesn't intend to do that; it seems just to happen. Disappointments, accidents, and bad people who selfishly take from others and do not care whom they hurt on their selfish journey are everywhere. But you get to decide with which people you want to surround yourselves.

"I've always believed that heaven and hell are not make-believe, faraway biblical metaphors but real. Both heaven and hell are here, right now, and you can choose to live in either. You determine how you treat others and if you will live in the light or in the darkness. My sweet daughters, sooner or later, you will see that the pen is in your hands, as you write the story of your life and the lives of your own family. Make it positive.

"The names of these six people won't mean anything to you, and in reality, I don't even know some of their names myself. Their deeds and generosity, or just their gentle presence, will have meaning, however; and you might recognize that our family life shifted direction after I encountered them."

But then he put the pen down. His mind just went into a fog. How much time did his wife really have? What was he doing sitting in the den? Why was he not with her constantly whether or not she was sleeping? What a fool he was! Nothing was more important to him than his wife's wellbeing and his time with her. He had made up his mind that they are on this journey together. Where it went, when it detoured, how it would end—or if and how it would begin anew—was to be a continuation of their joint story. They would face the next chapter together. That was the only way the future looked clear to him. They defined and completed each other. They had to take this final step as one.

He walked into the bedroom. It was no longer just a bedroom. It had become a time capsule. A temple. An altar. It reminded him of his time with the shamans in Peru. Of course. It was time to focus on Peru and the Indigenous elder. His mind raced to that experience.

The school for shamans in Pucallpa, Peru, was a sanctuary. A place beyond life and death. He had gone on his own fifteen years prior, feeling compelled to travel there—his wife didn't want to go to the jungle then. It was more than challenging to be there for ten days. He had entered a world that was unchanged since prehistoric times. The Amazon rainforest.

It seemed like he had always been interested in shamanism. He read about it in school in an anthropology course, and then on his own he studied its ancient practices. The shapeshifting. The journeys to enter the worlds of the spirit guides and ancestors, the upper and lower worlds. The power animals. The cloud dancers. It fascinated him so. To be able to enter a world of the spirit

THE HOUSE ON GENESIS ROAD

and leave behind the robotic, mechanized world most contemporary Americans have succumbed to filled him with excitement.

He had arrived at the school in a canoe carved by hand out of a tree truck. Two locals paddled it into the wilderness on the Ucayali River. There were four other travelers in the canoe with them who came from different parts of the developed, industrialized world. Like him, each was there for a personal reason. He wasn't entirely sure why he was there yet; he believed that whatever he learned would come in handy one day or shine a light onto a future path that he would need help traveling. Like now.

This was that day.

He had gone to Pucallpa seeking more of himself. Could he now tap into a quality from that trip which he had long ago buried? A hidden gift that only the shamans could unlock? Was there truly a place where time stopped, where his body would get a chance to remember that it had the knowledge and ability to cure itself? Where the leap could be made into the nonordinary realm?

He was looking for a way out of the horrible situation he and his wife were in. Traditional medicine and conventional medications were of little use against COVID. Maybe a spiritual remedy would be the only recourse to move them forward. So often the past holds secrets that unlock the future. Ancient and Indigenous wisdom might offer the solution he needed. What if he could guide them both—himself and his wife—on a shamanic journey to the other side, so they could stay there together after shedding their bodies?

He hoped he could remember the path to a higher dimension of reality that possibly awaited.

A long ago philosopher wrote that most people die spiritually long before their bodies fail. He never wanted to become someone who gave up on his dreams and lived a life of such routine that he was simply going through the motions. It is easy for the days all to seem to bleed into each other and for the magic and mystery of life to evaporate. Yet, he trusted that there was a universe of knowledge inside everyone and he was hungry to access it.

He believed we are not just passive travelers through life. That we possess universal consciousness, although the knowledge this affords us can be stripped away by our exposure to the constant noise and nonsense of 24/7 everything. And he felt sure he would have to go into the quiet to hear the clear voice of wisdom within his mind again.

He didn't want to miss the gifts that are all around us which he knew he so often walked past blindly. It was a constant battle for him to stay connected to the more. We have been conditioned to live in boxes, drive in boxes, work in boxes, shop in boxes. It is hard to see beyond the walls of the boxes we allow to define and confine us. Death is the ultimate box that defines us. From the day we are born, it haunts us and controls our choices.

The man went to Peru because he wondered if there is a way to move beyond the last fearful box of his beliefs. He did not want to accept a false narrative, especially if that narrative was just a means to keep control over him—and everyone—by making him fearful throughout his days.

To heal and cure himself through a spiritual reawakening was the enticement to Peru. *How do we define life? Where does the energy go? What happens to the soul? Is there a universal soul that unites us all? What is life/nonlife if everything is made of energy?* He wanted the answers to these and other questions.

One evening during his time in Pucallpa, an Indigenous elder took him aside and said he wanted to take him on a journey to the "upper world." He understood this to mean a higher plane of existence, an alternate dimension where you could meet spirit guides and teachers. *Maybe angelic beings?*

In shamanic circles, the other side is known as *nonordinary reality.* It is a realm you enter through ritual, and you are then present with the spirits. The curtain that separates this reality from the shaman realm is drawn to the side by ritual. Age is irrelevant. Time is no longer viewed as an overriding factor. In fact, time is shown to be the self-imposed trickster that we fear by fretting that we are limited to a certain amount of it and then we disappear.

Harmony is sought in the shamanic world.

According to the shaman's teaching, in the boxed world, we all live in disharmony. He was ready to travel the path to the world of the soul healers, a world where harmony was the universal language.

He hoped it truly existed. It had to exist. He no longer wanted to believe that the limitations of man could or would define the boundaries of the world around him. It was like asking an ant to opine about the cosmos.

The man was on to something. What we think about what there is and what there actually is are two entirely different things. The universe does not exist in a box or surrounded by walls. The universe is ever expanding. We are part of it. The most advanced deep space telescopes—the Hubble, the Webb—show us how we live in a vast and extraordinary universe, yet we too often squabble and rage about minutiae like finding a parking space on a city street. Smallness has become the big thing in our little inch of space.

The man's first conscious connection to the awesome, ever-expanding unknown was made on this evening in the Amazon jungle.

The elder said that when we dream, especially if we are consciously dreaming, we can connect with those who have passed from this life. We can also connect with the cosmos, as it is the very fabric of who and what we are and can be. We have just forgotten our true nature. He taught that it is possible to experience realms beyond the confines of what we, in modern society, believe is real because the body is merely a vehicle that we live in temporarily and then discard. The shaman took the man away from the rest of the group to a small tent further inland from the river. He was invited to lay on a soft pallet and relax. The elder then picked up a drum and began beating out a hypnotic rhythm. It sounded and felt like a heartbeat. As he closed his eyes, he felt like he was back in his mother's womb. He also sensed that there was some presence, like a "guide" there to assist him if needed.

The elder stopped drumming to go over to a small spineless cactus and cut a piece of it off. He learned later that it was peyote, a plant that contains the hallucinogen mescaline among other things. The elder told him that it was used for healing and spiritual visualizations. He ate it.

The "trip" he took that evening was beyond explanation. He danced in the clouds. He ran with the giraffes. He witnessed his own birth; and then experienced himself growing older but without aging. He saw that life never ends but just morphs into different energy fields. He learned that we are consciously present no matter what outward form or shape we take. And we are one with the beauty of all of life. He also came face to face with himself. It was as if he was staring into a living mirror looking into his own eyes which were looking back at him.

He wrestled with the question of why we permit the ugliness of some to rob us of the beauty that is our destiny. By the end of the evening, he was no longer a prisoner of the manufactured world created by the media and the money grabbers. He was liberated. He felt free from all constraints.

He had erased his own outline of form and shape. He had become more than his mere pieces. His soul had a voice. He had heard it. His soul became a tangible entity he knew in its own right. The idea of a soul was no longer theory or a philosophical discussion point for him. And he understood that the soul is more than the individual.

His soul was connected to universal consciousness. The history and the thoughts of all time were at his fingertips.

Some people say we must fear death in order to live at full throttle in the present moment. Although that liberates some to live boldly, fearing death is just another type of box in which people can become trapped. In fact, that which our soul, our energy, our being is connected to at all times is truly majestic. Life and death cannot sever the connection. We are always more than the present moment. We are colors in a rainbow of light traveling throughout the universe and existing in all of time.

During his trip, the man had this awakening. He felt fully alive, but more than that . . . he felt one with all of life . . . both tangible and intangible at once. The past, the present, and the future seemed to merge into one singular band of light, and he was traveling along that band of light and saw that he could go in any direction at his own choosing.

He had other mind-bending experiences in the jungle but this experience opened his mind and soul to the importance of smashing the limits we place on ourselves. The modern world wants to keep us engaged in a small tale of buying, selling, watching, being watched, and feeling afraid. He wanted none of that anymore.

The question was, could he continue on this path of creating a better reality that the elder showed him by taking him beyond the ultimate limitation? And could he tangibly experience not a world of life and death but one of eternal being?

He looked up at the sky and saw that we are all minuscule pieces of an unending story of creation. We are not visitors in the cosmic tale; we are integral parts of it.

The ten days in Peru went by in a heartbeat.

When he got home, the man tried to maintain the unlimited feeling of that evening and integrate the lessons of the elder. But as in most things, everyday life issues interfered with his best intentions. In the evenings, he would meditate on the deck. He even bought a Native American drum and downloaded audios of shamanic prayers and guided journey visualizations. Over time, however, he felt like he lost the "touch." He slacked off on doing his practices.

Until that day.

Then the memory of the elder brought it all roaring back in vivid detail.

If there was ever a time to recapture the power and connection to the "more" it was now.

He looked at his love and said, "We need to go on a journey together."

"Where?" she weakly asked.

"To the other side, my love."

She looked at him and a tear came to her eye, then she nodded. "Yes, take me there, please," she whispered.

"We will go there together. You are never alone," he replied.

He put on some of the audio recordings of visualizations that he had previously downloaded. For the next hour they listened, breathed, and journeyed to other worlds and times. They stayed connected by intertwining their fingers with each other.

After that hour he took his left hand and placed it on her heart. He could feel the beating of her heart. It was slow but strong. He asked her to keep her eyes closed, then closed his, and he said, "Let's slow our breath down. We will each breathe in gradually for an intake of a five count, hold our breaths for a five count, and then slowly breathe out for another five count. Keep doing this until I tap your heart."

The breathing exercise began.

Over the next five minutes, they both followed the process he'd outlined. At first it was difficult, but then something happened. Although they were becoming lightheaded, they also felt a warm, calm sensation come over them both. But even more than that . . . they did not feel like two individual people anymore. They were one being, connected in a way they'd never been before. They felt whole, complete, and beautiful.

Harmony seems so rare these days in a world that is at war with itself and everyone in it. Everyone is scrambling for whatever scraps, tokens, and prurient objects are the calling card or interest of the day. Social media has turned everyone into the emcee of their own event, which they are pretending is reality and relevant. For the man, none of it compared to the beauty of breathing in synchrony with the woman he loved.

Although science has taught us so much about the universe and our place in it, our thinking, in general, should be more advanced. Superstition and fear preclude advanced thinking. The current era is dystopic in a way never experienced before. We use our technology for prurient endeavors. We seem just to enjoy spying on each other, and then schadenfreude takes over. Mass hysteria and delusion have become the coin of the realm. For the man, it was time to break these bonds. It was time to seek the road that leads to a nonordinary reality known as the upper world. The spirit world. The world beyond the ordinary. This was the magical, mystical world to which the wise elder had introduced him.

But could he remember how to get there? Could the two of them learn the secret of mutual journeying? Could they enter the realm where life and death are irrelevant? Venture into a place where we are other than flesh and blood—more than what medicine says we are.

There had to be more. Doesn't there have to be more? All this creation. All this majesty. The mountains, rivers, oceans, trees, clouds, stars, moons, suns, galaxies can't be reduced in the end to some half-hour-long, bad talent contest or the nonsensical screaming match between talking heads on a cable program? If that were the case then why bother? The amazing creation that is us and our planet and the cosmos could not have been offered to us so we could squander it. It was time to look up, look out, and look beyond.

A thought sped through the man's mind. *That's it! We all have been hijacked by the loudest voices in the room. Not the wisest. Hijacked by the angry cries of the lost ones who pretend to be found. Not the guardians of the light. Rather by the denizens of the dark.*

It was time to join the wise ones. The guardians of the light. Break free of these chains. Heaven and hell. Garden of Eden or banishment. Satan, the Devil. God and salvation. Vampires, werewolves, and other monsters—or redemption. These are all in the world we create right now. But we still have a choice. Choose a world that makes us whole, not a world that tears us apart. It is time to choose the wise, harmonious path. Finally.

So, it is time to journey on and try to become part of what was originally intended. Find the original teachers before the pretenders take further control.

His hand was on her heart. She placed her hand over his. The drumming was getting stronger. It felt as if the smells in the room altered. There was a sweet aroma coming from ... well ... everywhere. Although the fan was spinning, but it seemed to go in fits and starts. Almost as if there was someone or something playing with it. The room felt cooler. Not cold. Not uncomfortable. Just a cool breeze like a cool island evening.

The room was lit by one nightstand lamp at this moment. This light began to flicker and then went off. The only light now was the natural light for that time of day. But time itself felt irrelevant. And so, at this critical moment in their lives, with their eyes closed, they each said to the other, almost at the exact same time, "Do you feel the presence?"

The shamanic elder in Peru had told him that if the journey were right and a spirit guide felt the honesty and urgency of the connection, one or more would appear.

And so just then a loving, knowing presence had appeared in the bedroom. How to describe what or who was there? It was more of a vision or a hologram than a human being—there, but not. This vision or entity had the form of a person in that it was bilateral with arms and legs, yet without features.

It opened its arms and began to speak. "My name is Agnam, your guide in spirit, and I have come to you to help you make a transition to another dimension of existence. What you need to know is that the only thing holding you back from attaining what you seek now is fear, and your own ideas of limitation. You are less afraid than most I encounter; however, your minds have to catch up with your hearts.

"Throughout their lives, people are always waiting for something to happen. At this stage in a life most are seeking the purpose or meaning of their time here. They think that some one thing will finally make their time here make sense or change things in a manner that will permit them to move on to a new chapter in the narrative of their existence. But this is narrow, myopic thinking. By focusing on these limited moments and defining their options through them, people put everything, including themselves in an even smaller container. They engage in self-limitation.

"You see, as soon as you narrowly define yourself and your options, you exclude the rest of what is possible, including that which seems like magic from your perspective as a corporeal being. You, in fact, voluntarily and even joyfully, sever yourself from the full majesty of the day, your relationships, your dreams, and the grandness of existence itself.

"But that is only part of what you miss. If you define your life itself as a here-and-now physical experience then you place the rest of what I am going to tell you about into the dreaded category of nonexistence. You decide that death is the end of your possibilities and it becomes a huge, horrible thing to fear.

"You must not allow fear to control you. Fear of death, fear of the unknown really, can consume you—and all because of your original error of believing in the boxes you have been taught to put yourself in.

"The limitations you learned are not true. You were never meant to be limited by anything in your world. This self-imposed isolation from your true nature and the amazing gift of existence and eternity is an illusion. A matrix of sorts. To attain what you seek, you need to shift your perception, but only slightly.

"You are an integral part of the universe. In fact, you *are* the universe. There is no duality. There is only the one. And you are parts of the one!"

The vision paused. It was surveying the two of them. They felt a bit lightheaded. The woman opened her eyes and looked at her husband. The man looked at his wife. They could see an inner glow in each other that shone from their eyes.

They did not know where they were any longer, only that they were not in the "old" world. They were in a new place. Their perceptions were entirely new. More pronounced. Colors seemed brighter. Sounds clearer. *Maybe,* they thought, *this is the world we were supposed to be living in all along.*

The man reflected on the idea of having been programmed. At least for him, it was true that he had for years conformed to be as "expected." When he was young he needed approval—this was normal, all children must learn how to survive in the strange world they enter. Life experience apparently has bookends. In the early years, people need to be fed, cared for, and housed. Later on, either due to the process of aging or an illness, such as his wife's COVID, the need to be fed, cared for, and housed returns. It's easy to assume that there is one narrative with the same arc for everyone. Years ago, he had chosen not to conform to this way of thinking.

But he had seen many other people become docile beings merely trying to survive. They settled so easily for crumbs instead of the banquet. Always playing the victim was one of the ways people he knew limited themselves. They grew attached in many instances to the smallest story available, of work, out of seeking recognition, money, or security. He'd narrowly avoided this trap.

Funny, he thought, *too many of us turn our power over to others, who, most of the time, could not care less for us. When did smallness become such a big deal?*

At the moment of their transition to something most people fear, the absurdity of it all was becoming clearer to the couple. Exactly what was the purpose and meaning of the short, minor journey on Earth, in a human body, given they lived in an infinite universe? Do people exist only for a few nanoseconds relative to the entire history of the cosmos? Is it always looking over our shoulders for the next catastrophe to creep up on us that causes us to lose sight of the fact that there is a before and an after in relation to our brief existence in a narrow form. Where were we before and where will we be after this? The prospect was enticing. They felt ready to go.

The man looked up at the vision and asked for more guidance. "Can there be a light to show us the way? Please."

And so Agnam began, "Your body is merely a parking spot for some of the energy of the cosmos. It was never intended to be more than this. You are both at the threshold of embracing a moment of clarity. Let go of any skepticism that your mind is clinging to protect you from acceptance of this moment in time.

"You are pure energy captured in a dissolving envelope. End your battle to preserve the envelope and your reluctance to undergo this transition, and focus on appreciating the pure energy that is you. Your future is before you. Your consciousness will survive the death of your bodies. Your essence will remain. It will not vanish. Only the envelope dissolves. So don't fret. Don't cry. Don't despair. It is silly to long for and mourn the passing away of the transitory when an everlasting reality awaits you.

"Your fear of separation from each other is just another idea of limitation you can release. The truth is that you can be with anyone you choose to be with by merely remembering your true self and opening your heart and soul to the cosmos that always was and is your destiny."

The vision paused and then continued, "This is enough for now. I want you both to take this all in and rest. I shall return soon. For now, simply allow yourself to feel into the 'more.' Once you do this, you will then be ready for immersion in the majestic story that is truly you."

Agnam was gone. The fan continued its normal spinning, and the flickering light went back on.

A silence filled the room. They each squeezed the other's hand and then released their grip on it. The man asked the woman to rest, saying he would be back soon. He said he wanted to write down his thoughts again, to help him process them. He was uplifted and told his wife that he was sure they had a long, exciting journey before them.

She asked, "Are you sure you want to do this? I mean— I am dying, but you could go on for many years."

He said, "There is nothing to fear." He then smiled and added, "You know I always wanted to part of this grand awakening." He believed this but was still being challenged by the enormity of the decision.

She closed her eyes and gave a gentle nod. Then she said, "I love you."

"Of course, you do," he responded and winked.

The man went back to the den. He picked up his pen and continued to write his last letter to Sarah and Rachel. He wanted to describe the six people who had changed him. Clearly, the elder in Peru was one of the six. But some earlier memories were more pressing at the moment.

"Sarah, Rachel, if you could travel back in time, where would you stop along the way? You can't change anything. You can't even nudge things in a different direction. But if you could observe and study one spot like you were doing a school project, is there one spot that you've always wondered about?

"I know where I would go if I could. It would be a moment in fourth grade when the teacher asked all the girls to stand up and introduce themselves on the first day of class. It was my first day in a new school and I knew no one. I was so busy putting my pencils

away in my desk and so nervous about being in this new school that I wasn't listening well.

"When I was young, we moved a lot, so I seemed always to be the 'new kid.' On this first day back after the summer vacation, everyone was talking to their friends and catching up, but no one was talking to me because they didn't know me. I saw kids starting to stand up and thought that must be what you do at the beginning of class in this new school. So, I proudly stood up to introduce myself to my hoped for new friends, and everyone started to laugh.

"At first, I didn't know why. Then I saw that only girls were standing. As I began to sit down, the teacher said not to. She said she wanted to turn this moment into a 'learning experience' and use me as an example about not paying attention. Cruelly, she called me Sally. I told her my name, and she said that couldn't be my name because that name was a boy's name. She said, 'You must be mistaken, Sally. Please tell us about yourself.' I was so humiliated that instead of intro-ducing myself, I hung my head and sat down. For the next two weeks, all the kids called me Sally.

"That teacher was heartless. Her treatment of me was cruel. It was especially sad since I had arrived with high hopes that morning. Up until then, my family was always on the move. But my parents had bought a house, so this home was hopefully going to be permanent. That was an incredibly painful event.

"If I could go back, I would want to revisit that moment in which I witnessed the cruelty of an authority figure. It taught me so much that to some extent it changed me indelibly. I learned that we arbitrarily give power to some who are undeserving of it. This is as unappetizing as the ease with which we mock and bully the innocent. But I also learned about

the inner voice that would give me the strength to shrug off arbitrary cruelty and move on. Or at least pretend to.

"To a great extent, that moment taught me that life can be unfair but that it does not mean I too have to be unfair to others. I learned that compassion is a good quality and empathy is critical. I carried those lessons forward in my life.

"That teacher, through her awful behavior, made me a more thoughtful person. Cruelty is easy. Generosity is tougher.

"In your own lives, I encourage you to seek the kind response. Don't jump to the ever so easy nasty side of life. Live with compassion and empathy. Be the thoughtful response to out-of-left-field cruelty when you encounter it. Always take the higher ground. You will sleep much better at night and not poison yourself by sending acid hatred coursing through your veins. Give yourself and others a break from being flawed human beings. I have always thanked that sad example of a teacher for the lesson."

He realized that he just recounted the story of the second of the six strangers who influenced him, but that he had never finished telling his daughters about the shamanic elder he met in Peru. He also wanted them to know about the encounter that had just taken place in the bedroom with Agnam. He tried to detail this as best as he could.

It was now past 10 PM. The hospice aide had arrived to spend the night hours with his wife. He walked in to kiss her good night. Tomorrow was going to be a big day. A day of transformation. It was going to be beautiful.

The man woke up early.

The sun was still not quite sure it was getting up. He walked into the kitchen to grab a cup of coffee. The hospice aide heard him and joined him in the kitchen. The aide said that it was a quiet evening and "his bride" was still sleeping. He told the aide that she could go home and he would take over. He thanked her as usual, and then walked into the bedroom.

As he entered the room, he contemplated the many basic questions that the pandemic had raised which we all try to avoid. For example, Where is the line between life and death? This thin, invisible line is as slight as a single, shallow breath.

There had been occasions when he sat with a friend or relative who was there and then not. There wasn't even a transition. No fanfare. No announcement. In one split second and one exhalation, they were gone. But gone where? And exactly *what* was gone? Each body was still there but its essence—the personality, the soulful glance, the joy, and the laughter, were not—except in his memory. Those qualities were not bound to the body. They were intangible and, he reasoned, must belong to some higher power.

If these intangible qualities persisted beyond death of the body, and the elder was right that they join some intangible dimension that is all around us, then there was nothing of which to be afraid. He could let go of any remaining reluctance to transition. But he was still struggling with the impact this would have on the girls and the grandchildren. If he told them his thoughts about this or decided to lay it all out in the legacy letter he had begun writing for them . . . well, either choice seemed bad to him.

And truthfully he still didn't know what he would do. He was trying to soothe his wife, and at the same time, didn't want to cause greater anguish to his family. But also, he had to be true to himself and his needs. The prospect of a future alone with the loss of his love constantly weighing on him was unbearable.

4. Clarity

His internal debate started to bring up more issues for the man but also began to put into order some of the confusion racing through him. This transition would not signify the ending of anything. This was a beginning. In the house on Genesis Road, it was always the beginning. It would always be morning. This transition was simply a metamorphosis.

His wife was still sleeping. He kissed her on the forehead and headed back to his writing in the den.

He picked up his pen. *How can I explain this to Sarah and Rachel?* he thought. He decided to say it as simply as he could.

He continued the letter:

"Loss is devastating. The loss of a loved one shakes your very foundation. Sometimes, I think, it is not only the immediate shock of the loss but the loss of the fantasy of what was supposed to be and never was, and the loss of the dreams of what could have been and no longer can be. But here is the truth. You must break through that learned narrative because it is not the whole story. The whole story is richer and so

welcoming. There is a power in connecting to the larger, more open story. It is as if your story resonates in a limitless way.

"I have an experience that illustrates this power.

"You hear a piano. Each note lingers long past when you think it will. That's sonic resonance. And people carry lingering energy too, as do cultures. I learned this in Nepal.

"I remember being in the Himalayas and wandering the dirt roads in the village of Namche. It is a mountain village in the Khumbu region of the Himalayas, about a two-day trek from the landing strip at the airport in Lukla. On Saturdays, there is a bazaar in Namche where people from all over the region come to buy and sell everything from spices, food, and garments to bells. I was there this one Saturday with your mom.

"As we strolled through the bazaar, we saw a man sitting on a ledge near a cliff overlooking the mountain range. The sky was bright blue. The air was clean and crisp. The man was slowly washing a single potato. He was lost in a meditation of executing this simple yet profound task. Your mom decided to wander to see what hidden treasures she could find elsewhere. But for some reason, I asked if I could sit next to the man. I don't know if he understood me, but he smiled, and I took that as a yes.

"I sat down and gestured to the potato. He picked up another one from a small box that was on his other side and handed it to me. And so, I sat there washing this one potato. Nothing more. Nothing less. The man and I didn't talk. We just did our 'chore' of carefully washing the potatoes.

"This gentleman then put his potato down and picked up a bell. It was actually two small, round

metal cymbals linked together by a leather strap. He held the leather strap between his thumb and index finger, balancing them. Then he slightly jerked his hand and one cymbal hit the other. The sound created was sharp, loud, and beautiful. It filled the air around us with a pleasant vibration.

"To my astonishment, the sound reverberated throughout the mountain range. The ringing of the cymbals seemed to last forever. The tone of the ringing slowly changed as it traveled throughout the mountains. It seemed to fill the entire village with beauty. All I could hear was this singular sound. The ringing was first very present and took over the mountain range. But then something amazing happened. With each second that passed, the sound grew softer but somehow, stronger. Soft and strong. It felt like the sound had turned into a river of music that was flowing in the valleys of the Himalayas.

"That was a true demonstration of the remarkable power of resonance. It was unending. It seemed to last and become part of the mountain range itself. It became part of the wind. Part of the sky. Part of the light. Part of life itself. I could feel the vibration enter my body and resonate throughout my very being. I felt it in my heart, my soul, my imagination. Fortunately, it was a beautiful energy, not a frightening energy. I was glad, and felt liberated from fear, listening to the sound of the cymbals.

"I must have sat there for over an hour. In that time, the man and I never talked. We just held the potatoes as I listened to the ringing that reverberated through-out the Himalayas after he struck his cymbals once. Was it an echo? Was it just bouncing off the edges of the mountains? Or, as I came to believe, did the chiming become a part and parcel of the very air we

breathe and the world we live in. I don't think it ever faded. I believe it still lives in the mountains and valleys of the Khumbu region to this day.

"I realized later that this was one of my greatest lessons. Being present. Recognizing that the energy we possess continues. It never vanishes. We must embrace the mountain range of our world and see how our lives are vital, continuing parts of it all. Perhaps most importantly, we must recognize that the 'sound' of our life energy continues. Our lives continue even beyond the traditional sense of it all. The ringing of our words, our thoughts, our love continue.

"The 'sounds' of our lives reverberate and continue.

"The man on the cliff was the third person who dramatically changed my life and yours, through me. You see, the lessons I learned from him are some of the lessons I've taught you over the years. Be present. Your actions, words, conduct will inevitably continue to influence others long after you move on. And never forget the ringing of the cymbals. They are still reverberating throughout the mountains."

He put down the pen, closed his eyes, and dozed off for a moment.

Where do we go when we sleep? Is it nothingness or is there something more going on at that moment in time? Is it like death? The man didn't believe that. Is it simply being unconscious? He didn't believe that either. He once went to a lecture on sleep and the secret world it opens. It was at the local community college. There were two speakers. One was a sleep specialist from the sleep disorder clinic in town. The other was a spiritual counselor who had studied sleep and its relationship to the subconscious mind and believed it even gave us a connection to the cosmos.

The sleep disorder specialist was interesting, but it was the spiritualist he came to listen to. He was mesmerized by the idea that when we sleep—with no sleep aids or drugs of any sort, and with the right preparation, or as he termed it, *incubation*—we can journey to the world from which we originally came and the place where we go once our tangible lives conclude. The lecturer called human life a *detour.*

He came to think of the lecturer as a guide to the other side. "It is not scary," the man had said, "there is nothing to fear. It is not nothingness. Rather a new horizon opens. We just can't access it now in our culture because we are blinded by the sights of the overly chaotic environment in which we reside." The spiritualist implied that people who live in harmony with nature can experience other worlds more easily than those who don't. However, it is possible for us to visit the "other world" in our sleep.

Hearing the lecture gave him that comfort about "what next" that so many fret and anguish about.

When the man woke from his nap at his desk, he headed back to the bedroom.

When your love is gravely ill, day and night become interchangeable. The sunrise and sunset are nothing more than momentary changes in color. Time takes on a life of its own. The sick room is mostly dark with some light sneaking in through the slightly drawn shades now and then. When the darkness/lightness of the day are so easily confused, it can disorientate you.

To give his wife's life some structure, the man tried his best to create signposts of sorts to separate day from night so sleep seemed more natural to her and she wouldn't feel like a sick person lost in a hospital wing. Some days it worked better than others. He wanted to make each minute matter. Daytime was the time when you did certain chores. He would ask her to hand him some dishes or glasses left over from the night before so they could "clean up the room" as if they were doing morning housekeeping. They would also tidy up the bed by straightening the blankets and sheets, and just do things that felt like morning things.

Later in the day, he would do evening-type things like lighting a candle and putting some classical music on to sweep away the daily concerns as best he could. He didn't know if it helped, but he figured it was something positive—and that was always a good thing.

It was getting tougher for her with each passing hour. The coughing, the congestion, the just plain feeling horrible. As to the coughing, she said it felt like razor blades inside her lungs. She really wasn't eating anymore. Each moment was precious and painful.

End of life is the most critical part of any marriage, a stage when time and love connect. Nothing matters anymore except holding on to your love. Wanting to go back in time. Wanting to begin again. Wanting more. Regretting letting moments slip away. Regretting moments of angry nonsense. Recalling the firsts of everything, such as their first meeting.

Facing the winding-down moments as life travelers, you just want to stop the clock. But you know you can't. You truly want to scream. So, how to deal with it all?

He concluded that you cope and keep devotion alive in your marriage by realizing that death is only the tangible part of your journey together. Although it is a narrow story within a broader story, it should be appreciated for its qualities. He wanted to meet physical life on its own terms but also was sure there was more to come. *There is no end,* he mused. *We've got to go beyond the lifetime of indoctrination that teaches us our physical lives are where we end. We've got to escape any worry we have about dying, as it's a box. I do not believe for a second that our marriage will be dissolved.*

He understood that each part of his cosmic story needed to be acknowledged, fought for, treasured, and extended for as long as it could be and never feared. Whether it was the here and now or the "there and after," he felt sure it would be available to their consciousness if they could prepare themselves adequately for the experience.

He often would find himself looking at his wristwatch, which he still wore out of habit despite carrying a smartphone in his pocket that knew everything about him, including the length of his stride, his heartrate, and his geolocation. He liked to gaze at the hands on the dial face, spinning around. The day had its way of flowing along. Each minute, each second, brought another earthquake of emotions. *We just can't stop the ticking of life,* he mused, then smiled.

The watch. The clock. What an invention that has taken over our lives! It quietly dictates all we do: When we rise. When we sleep, eat, work, exercise, and so on. It seems that it is just another creation that separates us from the natural order. From nature. No other creature lives by the clock. Why is that?

If we handed a watch over to a chimpanzee, it would just play with it, treating it like any other trinket. It would not run its life by studying its action as we do. But here the man was, checking his watch in order to see what time was left in the day. *A watch measures the time gone. The minutes lost. The hopes and dreams become yesterday. Crazy,* he thought.

He stopped himself, knowing he could get carried away.

Although the lines of time and space always seems to be present in all things and tasks we undertake, he discerned that it was now the right moment for him to erase those lines. He took off his watch and put it in the top dresser drawer. He felt some freedom once he had done that, a sense of being liberated from another of mankind's creations that too often prevent us from being present in each singular moment of our lives and give us the erroneous idea that we can control our days.

He took a deep breath and reminded himself to let go.

As his wife slept, the man sat in his easy chair across from her with his hands folded on his lap. He shook his head. Sometimes he did that when he was puzzled about how their lives were playing out. There always seemed to be a fork in the road. *Sooner or later, you have to trust your intuition, your instinct, your gut, and decide,* he told himself. There would be no turning back at that moment. Once the choice was made it would be irreversible. It was a sobering thought. Nothing fanciful about it at all.

He knew she was deathly ill. He knew she was not getting through this. It was so hard for the woman to breathe, yet she was keeping focused on being present in this last stage of this part of her journey. It was almost as if she wanted to appreciate even the sick part of her story because it was part of her being consciously alive.

From time to time, she would look at her husband as if she were studying his face. She would touch his lips and run her fingers over his cheeks and stare at him intently. She wanted to remember. He figured she had less than a few days to go before her body gave up. At these moments it was the water and a periodic protein shake that she would try to "get down" that had kept her going this long. But her appetite was not on her side any longer.

She would say that she wanted to be released. "Existing is not living. Existing is just a place holder for life. Not life itself," she would insist. And then, just a moment later, she would say she wanted to stay with him. It was a maddening time.

The man kept in touch with the girls about where the couple were in this moment in time. They kept sending their love. The grandchildren called also and asked him to tell Grandma how much they loved and appreciated her.

He walked into the bedroom to discuss the guide's visit with his wife and ask what she thought about summoning him back to guide them *both* to the other side. What did she think now about the prospect of him transitioning with her?

She said no one would understand. Sarah, Rachel, and the grandchildren would be doubly wounded by the loss of them both at the same time.

He said, "There is just no right answer."

She suggested, "Maybe we can do it in stages. Maybe you should join me after you comfort the girls and spend time with them telling them about the plan."

He told her they would never understand. And he even feared that they might want to seek some form of legal intervention, so he not "join" her. That they would view his death as suicide, the act of a bereft husband. He then mentioned that he was writing a letter.

"A what"? she asked.

"A letter."

"Saying what?"

He saw her getting upset and quickly explained that he was writing their daughters a letter about the love they had for each other and for them. He wanted the girls to know that this was a brutally tough decision but that he couldn't think of another way around this messed up situation and he was leaving them a sort of roadmap to where they would be and how the two of them believed they would always be there for them.

She nodded and gave him a weak smile.

She had always been the more pragmatic one of the two of them. In keeping with this, she frequently would say things like "Life is what you make it" and "Once it's over, it's over. There is no here, no there, no hereafter. There is above the ground and below."

Or, as she wished her body to be cremated, she'd say, "Ashes to ashes."

He, on the other hand, was always the one to say there had to be more. There had to be another chapter to the human story. That was why he spent time with shamans and Buddhist monks, studied in Hindu temples, and prayed in churches and synagogues. Whenever they traveled to a foreign country, he always steered the family to wander through, and sit a while in religious temples.

There was a 4 AM breakfast ceremony at a Buddhist temple in Cambodia, and reading from *The Tibetan Book of the Dead* in Nepal. Praying in the church in Positano, Italy, and standing in awe at the American cemetery in Normandy, France. These and so many more experiences had convinced him that there had to be more.

The two of them would talk about this prospect regularly. He knew his wife humored him about his beliefs in the main—but could all these faiths, spiritual writings, and religious people throughout history and around the world be so wrong?

Whether to a higher plane of existence or merely as atoms colliding, our energy must go somewhere when we die. He had faith that God or a grand force of some kind would ensure it. For him, the question was if we would be aware of the more to come. Would our consciousness still be present no matter what form or nonform we took?

The fork in the road of choice had arrived. He was truly tortured by this decision. Any choice he made he felt would be hurting another. There could be no do overs once this decision was made. He knew he must decide soon what to do. But first he needed to finish his letter. He was determined to complete the list of six helpful strangers that he had started.

Finding himself with pen in hand, he began again.

"The impactful encounters. The moments that redirect your life. Most of the time, these are not planned. Nothing is on the calendar. It is chance. Unintended. Sometimes you don't even catch the name of the person when their comment or gesture or response resonates with you. And sometimes it isn't even directed at you. You may just be a witness to a moment that somehow captures your attention and imagination. Then, maybe not immediately, but in time, you catch yourself being redirected in your life because of that moment.

"The fourth person I want to tell you about is someone whose name I never knew. I had just finished arguing a case one afternoon in the criminal court in downtown Bozeman. This had to be over forty years ago. It had been a long day already. I don't recall the details of the case, but I remember it was a very intense hearing. My client was wrongly charged. I remember that much. The evidence the state had was suspect at best and more circumstantial than direct.

In fact, nothing directly tied my client to the alleged crime. He seemed to be at the wrong place at the wrong time.

"I was arguing a motion to exclude certain evidence that would have resulted in the state's case being vivisected. The motion was getting heated and the judge, a former prosecutor, was ignoring the substance of the motion and summarily denied it. The effect of that ruling meant a most likely innocent man was going to be dragged through the justice system with the end result being uncertain. It was a brutally rough day in court for my client and incredibly frustrating for me.

"I packed up my files and headed out of the courtroom feeling despondent. I wasn't despondent for myself. I had won and lost hearings before. But I was upset for my client because I knew what he was facing. The cost, the time, the effects on his family and his employment were all weighing on me. Also, the uncertainty of the outcome always haunted me.

"I guess I got about halfway down the hall on the seventh floor of the criminal courthouse—I was headed to the bank of elevators—when there was a tap on my right shoulder. I turned around and saw a mountain of a man standing there. He had a suit on, and I figured he was a lawyer. His smile lit up the corridor. His eyes were sparkling and animated in their own way. He said . . . 'You are right! You are really good. Don't be discouraged. Keep the faith. Get back in there another day with a variation of this motion. You got this,' and then he turned and walked away.

"I never got his name. He didn't tell me. I just smiled, shook my head, and told myself that life can surprise you. There are some folks who will run down the hall

to offer a kind word of encouragement to another . . . even a stranger.

"I did reframe the motion and reargued it weeks later and was successful. But this lesson is not about that fact. This is about stepping out of your own worldly issues, your own daily problems and worries about different events, so that when you see someone else who needs a thumbs-up or a pat on the back of encouragement you can go there and be present with them in their moment. A kind gesture at the right time can change a life.

"We are all in different stages of change and sometimes need to see a smile or hear an uplifting comment to put life in context so we can move past our latest obstacle.

"I remember standing in line at a Starbucks one day. There was a woman just ahead of me. When she reached the counter, the young woman taking her order commented that she hadn't seen her in a while. The customer smiled, chuckled, and then responded that she had been 'swimming in the sea of change.' Swimming. What a great metaphor for the unexpected challenges in life. Not fighting the currents. Not being defeated by a single event. Not letting one person or authority figure rob you of your destiny and choices. Not giving up or giving in. Truly being present and putting each moment in the context of the grander story.

"Don't be run over by a single negative event or by negative people. Don't question your own integrity. Your own decency. Your own decision to meet life on your terms.

"Sometimes we all just need a silent nod. We have to accept that we are constantly swimming in a sea of change and be flexible and never be stuck in a

particular position or strident pose. That is what that stranger taught me when he tapped my shoulder in that hallway. Be the encouraging one in someone else's life. The ebb and flow of life permits you to adjust, adapt, and then overcome the latest challenge.

"I am so proud of both of you. You both have grown up to be strong, independent, caring people. Each of you has had your tests. Each of you has weathered some rough seas. Accept the encouragement from a stranger. Be the one to help another when you see that a kind word is badly needed. Be the one to reach out. Never forget that we all need that unexpected tap on the shoulder to reset our inner compasses."

He put the pen down. He was struggling so. He felt terrible that he would leave the girls without a family gathering. And yet, he hoped that Sarah and Rachel would read his letter and better understand the choice he was contemplating.

He knew that without his wife he would wander lost through the world. Oh, he would meet with friends and family, but he would be the third or fifth wheel at their gatherings. The obligatory invited one to a dinner. He was so set in his ways. And he was just too long down the road with her to think about beginning anything again. Nor would he even want to. There was no one else who could compare with her. True. Authentic. Genuine. Honest. Oh, she had her moments! But don't we all?

He was no prize. She understood him and accepted him for the challenged human he was. They'd established a rhythm in their life together. Even after all this time, she still made him want to be in harmony with her. They had grown up together.

The more he thought about it, it was becoming clearer that leaving with her wasn't a hard call. Living without her seemed like a barren landscape of just mere existence and nothing more. He thought that he would just end up being the invisible one at any social event.

What is a life without the most meaningful person you know being there and loving you?

He just came to understood that we are always present, whether in a tangible or intangible way, but to experience these realms together seemed to him to be where he wanted to be. Besides, they had never gone anyplace new without wanting to share the new adventure with each other.

He knew in his heart the path to travel—the road was there—and continued his letter. The question was how to ensure that he explained it effectively to Sarah and Rachel.

"Sarah and Rachel—now for the fifth person.

"I saw her out of the corner of my eye. I was driving south on Main Street, heading to a business meeting early one Monday morning, when I stopped at a red light. My mind was preoccupied with the topic of the meeting. Yet something about the scene caught my attention. Let me see if I can describe it as best I can.

"Why is it that some things just seem so critical yet, on reflection, they are not all that vital? It seems that so much of life is like that. Small, nonsense, faux, emergency stuff crowds out truly important stuff and then regrets settle in. And sometimes events that seem so insignificant that they're not even worthy of a second thought, on reflection, turn out to be some of the most compelling, life-shifting moments you could

ever experience. That happened to me this one morning.

"What I saw was no small thing. It might seem that way to others, but stayed with me and made me a better person. That sounds so crazy, considering I watched the moment unfold in the span of a red light on Main Street.

"That is the mystery of time. A split second can change you for better or worse and become the foundation of your life. Never forget this, girls. One glance can be more critical than a month of meetings or a year of relationships.

"Sitting at that light, I turned my head and saw a little girl with a limp. One leg was shorter than the other and she was trying to keep up with her mother. I surmised that her mother was trying to get to the corner to cross the street before the light changed. There was a bus stop on the other side of the street, and she didn't want to miss the bus.

"The girl's mother was fumbling for coins in her purse to get out the right change to pay the bus fare. (This was still before buses had card readers.) Although the woman was clearly harried and already exhausted even before the day truly started, I had the sense, from looking at the little girl's smile, that the bond between mother and child was unbreakable. I could feel the love between the two of them. The innocence of the little girl was palpable. She radiated joyfulness and giddiness.

"The little girl was giggling and holding one red balloon. The balloon had the name of some hardware store or another on it. A shop owner probably gave it to her when her mom stopped off there on the way to the bus stop. The little girl (I will call her Rebecca) seemed so excited to be walking on Main Street with

her mom, holding the balloon, and racing to get through the crosswalk before the green light turned red, that she wasn't focused on her limp. I doubt Rebecca thought of herself as 'disabled.'

"In my head, in that instant I saw her, I created a world for Rebecca and her mom where Rebecca was loved purely for who she was and how she was, limp and all. I created a world where her mom always told Rebecca that she was perfect no matter what.

"Sometimes what seems like a disability to an outsider may very well be the gift that opens up a gentler world for all involved. I don't think Rebecca thought anything other than that she was on Main Street with her mom. She was wearing a bright yellow dress, white ankle socks, and shiny black leather Buster Brown shoes and she looked happy and adorable to me.

"Rebecca's mom got to the corner and saw the light turn yellow. She stopped and looked dismayed. The bus was pulling up and Rebecca was way behind because of her limp. Her mom looked down and then did this: She knelt down and held her arms out to Rebecca. She made not a sound. Not a 'hurry up.' Not a 'come on.' Not a 'We are going miss the bus and be late.' None of that. Just a smile and open arms.

"Rebecca did her best, smiling and giggling all the way. Walking down the street was an adventure to her. The beauty of it was that this was a day with her loving mom. It was Main Street. It was a balloon. It was the challenge of catching the bus. It was the excitement of meeting people on the bus. It was the thrill of showing everyone on the bus her red balloon.

"Rebecca got to her mom just as the light turned red and the bus pulled up. Her mother gathered

Rebecca into her arms and then looked up . . . at me in my car.

"The light had just turned green. A car honked a horn behind me. There were no cars on the opposite side of the street waiting for the light, nor where there any cars driving on the opposite side of the road at that moment. I looked at Rebecca and her mom, smiled, and motioned for them to cross the intersection to catch the bus.

"It was at that exact second that Rebecca looked at me. Our eyes met. Her eyes sparkled. She waved to me and then lifted her red balloon higher, so I was sure to see it. I waved back and gave a thumbs-up, pointing at the balloon. Rebecca again giggled and I sensed an old soul in that young little girl.

"They made the bus and I felt joy.

"That was it. Nothing more. Nothing less. Yet it has stayed with me forever. The question is why.

"Rebecca couldn't have been older than six years old. Her hair was long, dark, and braided. She was wearing that bright yellow summer dress. She was walking the whole way a few steps behind her mother until her mom's open arms embraced her. Her mother looked weary to me, but never showed a weary face to Rebecca.

"Over the years as I have reflected on that encounter, I guess it affected me because of the unconditional love I witnessed. But it was also Rebecca and her energy or spirit. She wasn't beaten down by her leg, her limp, her physical limitations, that I suspected over time might take its toll on her or cause others to bully her or treat her badly. But maybe not. Maybe the love of a mother for her precious daughter would overcome the harsh moments of life.

"Sarah, Rachel, that is the same love as you receive from your mom. That is her love for you. Never fear. Never fret. Her arms always were and always are and always will be open to you. And that woman is also who you both became as moms. You love your children with an open heart and open arms. You had the best role model ever.

"Never miss the moments to open your arms to help the one falling behind. There will be another light to catch. For me I might have been five minutes late to a meeting. For Rebecca and her mom, it was a moment of love, commitment, and a treasured experience. Life is just a collection of such moments. The combination of those singular moments create the finished portrait of a life.

"Don't be so self-absorbed that you miss the sweet, innocent times of your lives. Those are the moments that remind you that there is a critical place for gentleness and a warm embrace so needed these days."

He paused. Then, added:

"This little girl was the fifth person who impacted my life, and then yours. From her, I learned to slow down. To not hurry through the day. To not wish away any moment especially when I am with those I love. Keep the Rebeccas close to your heart. Keep an open heart. Don't let the ugly people in any day steal your joyfulness and stifle the giddiness of being alive now surrounded with those you love."

He put his pen down. He thought about how cruelty has become the coin of the realm these days. Everyone seems to have lost patience with each other. Everyone has the feeling that the game is rigged. Short temporal gains have become more important than the long-term benefits that take time to appear.

Maybe that was why his Rebecca moment had stayed with him. The joy of a child untainted and uncorrupted by the dark side of human nature. Her mom clearly only treated Rebecca with kindness and love. As he drove to his meeting on that particular day, he said a prayer that the rest of the world would be similarly kind and gentle with Rebecca. He prayed the sun would shine on her and let her live in a state of grace. Let her live in a world of gratitude. Although Rebecca couldn't change her physical condition, that didn't mean she should live a life of anger, frustration, disappointment, and the feeling of being less because of a physical disability. She was a child of God and evidently a vessel of joy and love to those around her.

He believed that her gentleness, sweetness, and kindness are what the world needs. She would probably shine a light for others with various challenges. But he knew a lot of able-bodied people who were emotionally and spiritually challenged. Maybe she would shine a light for them too.

He sat back in his chair and looked around the room. He noticed some mail on the desk addressed to him. He stared at the 1318 Genesis Road address. Of course! This gave him even more comfort regarding his upcoming decision.

When they bought the house on Genesis Road and gave it a specific number—1318—he didn't realize until much later the full significance of it. Yet, as the years went by, the entire family felt a subtle but clearly perceivable change come over each of them. A calm. A feeling of having a connection to a higher calling. A sense that they were living in a sanctuary that was a refuge from any darkness of the day. A home that they felt safe and secure in. The family knew they could trust each other. They knew that they would be always there for each other and were connected to a higher force.

One evening, he sat down with his wife and the girls and told them that he was reading up on numerology and angel numbers. He wanted to understand other possible meanings of 1318 beyond the biblical one they already knew. Since they lived inside this number, so to speak, and saw it every day as they left home and came back, he wanted to know more about their home's impact on each of them. Was there something the house brought to them as the current owners that was unique to it and them? Once again the house on Genesis Road was impacting the family.

Well, he learned that the number 1318 has many positive meanings. It was an *angel number.* He spent the evening reading to them all the positive messages he had found for 1318. The experience was uplifting and supported his belief that their souls were intertwined and they would be together forever and in fact the house was an integral part of their journey.

This was well before his wife became ill. But they learned that their soul separation from each other at any point during this tangible part of the journey would only be temporary. Once the physical part of their human story was written, they would reunite in the soul zone of existence.

He tried now to remember why 1318 supposedly had so much power. Then it came back to him: Whether taken as one number or divided into its parts . . . 1-3-1-8 or subparts like 13, 131, 18, 318, or adding them together to total 13, the meaning of the number pointed to self-reliance, focus, independence, balance, wisdom, gratitude, and nothing standing in their way to accomplish what they each choose to do.

Given this, now more than ever, his decision seemed right and true to where he and his wife both were at this moment in time. The original concept still rang true.

> *"Then Abram removed his tent, and came and dwelt*
> *in the plain of Mamre, which is in Hebron, and built*
> *there an altar to the Lord."*
> GENESIS 13:18

Their family lived in a sacred place on the planet. They were rooted. He knew well what this meant. He remembered seeing a beautiful painting in an art gallery in Positano years earlier of a mother with her two daughters. Beneath where the daughters were sitting in this painting, there were exposed roots in the ground. Both daughters were strongly rooted. He thought this meant that not only were they rooted to the earth—their cosmic home—but also that their mother had raised them to embrace positive core values. He liked to think that Sarah and Rachel were like those daughters. Strong and rooted. They were no pushovers for anyone or anything.

In the painting, the mother was blindfolded. He thought that meant that although the future was unknown it was just fine with them because they knew who they were and had defined themselves. He imagined they lived fearlessly, understanding that nothing is promised to anyone and this is the way life is intended to be. There are no warranties or guarantees in life. That is its nature.

He hoped his daughters would never forget they were linked to the universal moral compass that is available to all of us if we will only put aside the silliness of momentary fads or the immediate ego thrills that some charlatan is peddling to us.

He had always believed that Genesis was a special place. Everything pointed to that truth. But if he needed any additional guidance, support, reassurance, or comfort as to his upcoming decision, all of the angel number messages affirmed the wisdom of the choice.

The house at 1318 Genesis Road, his altar to God, was meant to be theirs.

He began to write again.

> "*We are all time travelers. We simply forget this truth. We are so used to living from day to day and being consumed by each day's events that we forget that we are more and are part of an ever-expanding universe. Mount Everest taught me that. That moment of sitting on the edge of a cliff in the Himalayas listening to the soundwaves of cymbals reflecting back to me from the horizon and beyond gave me a glimpse of the potential of being part of the flowing waves of life itself.*
>
> "*But if we are time travelers, if we can revisit past moments or experience future events, how do we enter that medium.*
>
> "*I am beginning to believe that our souls are the part of us that travels through time, a phenomenon which occurs the moment we relieve ourselves of the enveloping boxes that contain our souls. We have locked our souls up in our bodies all these years so we only get glimpses of our soul and its potential from time to time. There is so much we just don't understand. For example, have you ever seen a beautiful bird land in your backyard that was never there before? Haven't you seen a fleeting image or*

shadow of a lost loved one who appeared at the exact right time to comfort you? A song comes on that is 'your song' when you need it the most? The unexplained flickering lights in the house. Those aren't just coincidences. Those are real. Those are souls . . . intangible entities or energies . . . visiting you.

"Remember, no one is ever gone. No one is never not-here. Simply because they are not visible to your eyes doesn't mean they are not visible to your soul. You can always talk to me or your mom. You will just know when we are there with you. Talk with us. As you do that more and more, our connection should be easier. Our presence will be strengthened because we feel acknowledged and accepted. We just may be there in other forms or shapes that you must be open to— perhaps a winged being, like a bird, a butterfly, or a dragonfly.

"The way this happens, I believe, is that souls who've been liberated from their bodies understand that you have opened a doorway from one world to the next for them. It's like the sliding glass doorway in your kitchen. None of us hits a wall at death, rather we slide the separating door open. Death of our bodies is not the end. Death is the new beginning.

"Souls can acknowledge the ongoing relationship they have with you. You can feel them. You can see them with your inner eye. Therefore, you can reach out to Mom and me. We will never be gone. We will always be here with you to guide you."

He wanted Sarah and Rachel to know they would never be alone because love never dies. Love is eternal.

Hearing him in the den, the hospice aide called out to him. The aide sensed that he had been writing something because she would hear him talking to himself periodically. She asked him to please come into the bedroom.

As he walked in, he saw the aide sitting beside his beloved. The aide said, "Look at this."

At first, he wasn't certain what he was to look at, but then he saw why he was called in. His wife was sitting up in bed and looked so fresh and alert. It had to be two or three in the morning. He was puzzled.

He asked the aide if she could leave them alone for a few minutes. She said, "Of course," and stepped out.

"Hey, my love. What is happening?" he asked.

"I was there," she said, "and it was beautiful. It was everything I thought it would be. But I couldn't find you."

He was truly puzzled. *She was there?* Then he figured, *She must have been dreaming.*

It was as if she heard his thinking. She said, "I wasn't dreaming."

"Where were you my love?" he asked.

"I was on the other side . . . home. But I came back because I wanted to be there with you. I was lonely for you."

He held her hand and kissed her forehead. "We will be there soon, my sweet girl," he said. "Go back to sleep and I will make the final plans I just have a few more things to do."

She smiled and slid back in the bed. She threw him a kiss and closed her eyes.

He asked the aide to come back in and he headed for the den. Time was short. He needed to finish the letter to the girls. He didn't think they will ever understand but he had to try.

There was the sixth stranger. Maybe the most influential one of them all.

5. The True One

He didn't know how exactly to begin the next part of the letter. He has studied many different religions and philosophies but only a few fully registered with him. He'd been introduced to the poems of the thirteenth-century Sufi mystic Rumi when he traveled through Big Sur years earlier. He was at the Esalen Retreat Center when he heard a number of folks reading different quotes from the book *The Essential Rumi* to one another. It sounded so intriguing that he picked up the book and couldn't put it down.

Rumi's words subsequently led him to read more about the Sufi faith and the whirling dervishes. He was so captivated by what he was learning that he suggested to his wife that they travel to Istanbul. The whirling dervishes have a long, strong spiritual history in Turkey. He and his wife traveled all throughout Turkey for about a month. Near the end of the trip, they settled in in Istanbul.

He picked up the pen and began.

"It was early evening. Your mom and I were in Istanbul. We had already been there for about ten days. We had seen all the sights and sounds of this

wonderful, ancient part of the world. The city is half in Europe and half in Asia. You easily wander from culture to culture and absorb, not only the beauty of the different sections of the city, but the history and its impact on what life is and what it can still be. There is a richness to the marketplaces, the boulevards, and the small corner shops and cafes.

"But there was one particular reason we were there. We were there to witness a ritual of the Sufi Muslim order known as the Mevlevi Brotherhood. I thought I read that Rumi founded this brotherhood. Our hotel clerk gave us directions to the hall where the dervishes' ritual took place.

"As we entered the room, we saw chairs encircling a wooden floor. There were another fifteen to twenty people present besides us. The whirling dervishes entered wearing long, flowing, white robes and white, cone-shaped hats on their heads. They positioned their feet and toes just right in the wooden floor. I could tell that the positioning was intentional and important to the ceremony that was to soon begin. As the music started, they would spin from left to right on their left foot. The robes would be dancing with the movement. It was hypnotic. The whirling got faster and faster. Images began to blur. I was being hypnotized by the flowing robes, the spinning, the music, and the joyful celebration. Mystical. Magical. I got lost in the beauty of the dance. It would go on for ten minutes. We watched the dancers do this three times in a row with only a brief pause between dances.

"As an audience member seeing the dervishes, you get drawn into their experience. You want to release yourself from the confines that others try to bind you to. You want to rip away any negative thoughts. You feel one with the movement and the music. You almost

forget where you are. The present/past/future times evaporate. Eventually, you are simply present in the eternal moment. Watching them, my mind raced to the rhythm of Rumi. His poetry filled my mind and heart.

"I had been reading the writings of Rumi ever since Esalen years earlier. I loved his powerful, inspirational, thoughts about life, death, fear, love, and enlightenment. Rumi's poetry has always taken me, since then, to a center place in myself that I had never accessed at any other time previous to that until I was with the shamans.

"Rumi writes about releasing the ego. A releasing of the confines of the boxes and self-imposed envelopes we all find ourselves in. How it feels to strip away the shackles of everyday obligations and reveal the soulful part of this journey.

"From the elders of the shamanic world and the Sufi whirling dervish world, I gained a sense that the attainment of enlightenment was not only a hopeful intent but a reality.

"Sarah, Rachel, none of us ever becomes less by dying. As I spent time with both the shaman elders and the whirling dervishes and by listening to the music/drumming and being present in my body, mind, and soul, I was liberated and found I could ascend to the place I was always meant to be. There is nothing to fear.

There are just so many different paths to help us find peace and meaning to what so often feels like an isolated lonely journey. Even if we are alone, we don't have to feel lonely. Remembering each experience he'd had made him realize that there is always so much more to do, see, feel, and connect with. He also realized that music itself was a healing impact. He saw this, not only through his recollections of hearing the chime of the cymbals reverberating through the Himalayas and the sacred chanting of the whirling dervishes that helps them grow closer to God and spread divine energy throughout the world, but also with a quiet guitar as he sat in his den writing. The music tapped into another dimension of reality.

"After our incredible evening experience watching the dervishes whirl I was wide awake and energized. I told your mom that I just wanted to stroll the side streets of Istanbul for a while. She cuddled up with a book at the hotel as I walked from section to section of the wonderful, colorful city.

"There were a few musicians playing jazz on a corner by a cafe. Two guitarists and a keyboardist. I grabbed a coffee from the cafe and sat on a bench in the center of the boulevard to listen. The evening events had filled my heart with a blissfulness that is hard to describe.

"I didn't know how much time passed only that it was getting very late. The street was slowly becoming more deserted. It was then that I saw a clown walk by. Yes, a clown. I didn't know where he came from. Some show? Some carnival? Some odd private club somewhere on the boulevard? It didn't matter to me. There he was.

"The clown had a mouth painted red and shaped in a smile with sad eyes and a few dark tears running down his cheeks. I couldn't tell whether the tears were painted tears or real tears turned dark by streaming through the makeup around his eyes. He stopped, looked at me, waved, and then turned around and looked into the window of the cafe, which, at this time

of night, had become like a mirror. He took a handkerchief out of his back pocket and began to wipe away the clown makeup on his face. I watched him wipe away the disguise that he had painted on earlier. He did it very methodically and deliberately. With each layer of makeup gone, more of his face was revealed.

"Between wiping away the mask with the cloth and then applying the creams and oils he carried in a small bag to address a few remaining spots on his face, the clown's cleanup took about twenty minutes. When he was all done, he turned to me and bowed and I saw that he was a she. And she was this beautiful young woman. Truly stunning.

"I smiled and nodded to this woman to kind of say, 'Well done.' She nodded and smiled back. Then she came over to the bench I was sitting on and, in perfect English, asked if she could sit down for a while. I said, 'Of course.'

"I asked her where she was coming from. She told me that she wasn't coming from anywhere in particular. She told me she did this regularly. I asked, 'What do you do regularly?'

"She said that she would put on a mask some evenings and walk the boulevard until she saw someone she thought might need to witness her transformation. A metamorphosis of sorts.

"I asked, 'Was that person who you thought might need to see the possibilities of metamorphosis me tonight?'

"She said she wasn't sure, but she felt it was.

"We then talked for about an hour. She explained that everyone wears a mask. Some more obvious than others. The mask may be one of a garish clown or jester, a handsome rogue, a pretty damsel in distress, *a victim, a hero, a villain, or a savior. There are all kinds of masks and disguises people wear in our daily lives.' The problem with masks and disguises,' she told me, 'is that you forget who you are and what you really look like and what dreams you still have that are lost under the layers of makeup.'*

"*She also said, 'You lose touch with yourself. You become a stranger in your own skin. You forget that you are your own best friend. Your own best adviser. You forget that only you truly know yourself, because you can't see the identifying marks of yourself after fastening the mask in place. You start doubting yourself. You became afraid of taking your own advice. You started listening to others about what you should do in your own life.'*

"*We spoke about how those others can take up residence in our minds. They are the voices we hear. But we must choose. We must find our voices again. The choices. The decisions. These are ours to make.*

"*Many advice-givers can't figure out their own lives, yet believe they know how to tell us how to live ours.*

"*The woman said, 'Each morning when you wake up, greet yourself. Introduce yourself to yourself again. Seriously. Look in the mirror and welcome yourself into the new day. A day that is promised to no one but here it is waiting for you. You are not a prisoner of yesterday. You cannot be defined by anyone else. But you must choose wisely and with knowledge that you are worthy of the day. You see, you are the true one in your life, the one you have been waiting for.'*

"*After that, the clown stood up, smiled, and said, 'Thanks for listening to me.' I nodded and said, 'Thank you.'*

"Your mom and I left Istanbul a few days later.

"Never forget that you are your own best friend. You can rely on yourself. Trust your instincts. Keep growing, studying, learning, and fearlessly facing each day knowing who you are and that you are good with yourself.

"The sixth stranger you have to meet and come to terms with is you. You are the stranger in your own skin whom you must befriend, and once you are one with this stranger, you will finally be whole.

"I met that stranger late in the evening in Istanbul. That stranger has been traveling with me ever since. The stranger taught me that life is infinite.

"Whether healthy or ill, never forget that life continues. Life does not die. Life just transitions. Life transforms. Life is in a state of constant metamorphosis. Images may shift. 'Makeup' may come off. Time may move forward. But change never stops. There is always a new morning. And it is always beautiful in the morning.

"We love you so. Always have. Always will."

He put the pen down. He was weary. He reflected on Istanbul, Rumi, the whirling dervishes, and the clown. What a strange mixture of people, emotions, images, and enlightenment!

He thought about the unnamed people, the kind strangers, the fleeting moments that can change a life. The unexpected encounters that totally shift your life from one path to another. He thought about all the people we don't meet because we haven't stepped out of our comfort zone and taken risks. And he realized that risk is an important element in life. Being a bit uncomfortable may be one ingredient that is needed in each life.

He also now decided that he was going to reintroduce himself to himself and have the conversation he had been delaying. The what next. The next decision that was irreversible. He walked into the bathroom and looked in the mirror. He studied his face. His age and the stress of these days were etched on his face. He smiled at himself. Nodded. He knew what he was going to do . . . finally. He had a long talk with the "sixth stranger" and finally felt calm, both serene and accepting of where fate had brought him and his wife. He was comfortable in his own skin.

It was now close to morning. He hadn't slept a bit.

He went into the bedroom and told the hospice aide she could leave. He would take over. He decided that this was going to be the day that they would make their leap.

He had a few more things to tell the girls, and then Agnam, their spirit guide, would need to be summoned again for support. He looked at his bride. She was sound asleep. She looked like the little girl from her elementary school pictures around seven or eight years of age. Even now, even as sick as she was, there wasn't a wrinkle on her face. She was always like that though. Age did not register on her. She seemed to be a constant in a universe of change. He always believed that her inner peace and kindness reflected on her face.

He remembered reading Oscar Wilde's classic novel *The Picture of Dorian Gray*. The story is of a handsome young man who stays forever young even as his picture becomes ugly and grotesque because of his amoral and murderous ways.

He'd always believed that his bride was the antidote to Dorian Gray's plight. She stayed forever young because of her kind thoughts, her moral code, and her pure decency. Her appearance in photos from long ago and her present-day appearance were remarkably similar. He figured that a kind heart could do that.

He looked down at his sleeping girl in the bed and felt admiration for her, and appreciation that she had decided to travel the road of her life with him. And now he had decided to take the last step of hers with her. He couldn't let her transition alone. He couldn't think of her being scared and alone. They would hold each other and begin the metamorphosis.

6. Metamorphosis

He walked out onto the deck overlooking the mountain range. It was morning.

It's always beautiful in the morning, he thought.

As he looked out over the field, the dry riverbed, the bridge, the prayer flags, and the Buddha statue, his eyes kept moving to the horizon and upward. He took in the clouds, the morning light, and, in the distance, a pale moon that was lingering over the Montana skyline. He was witnessing infinity right in front of him. Infinity.

He laughed as at a private joke. *Why is it that the human race considers itself so wise and all-knowing, yet we only focus on the finite temporal images?*

Somehow, as soon as we became able to form words and sentences, name things, and solve riddles, we must have concluded that everything around us was created for our amusement, because we believed these capabilities made us wise, thoughtful, and all-knowing. We are such linear-thinking creatures, he thought.

We mastered the art of entertaining ourselves, but with the most juvenile of images and stories. There always seems to be the latest cartoon of superheroes and supervillains numbing the senses of us all. The stories are all the same, the images are all alike, the beginnings and endings of them seem interchangeable, yet we keep going back to see these stories because . . . , he pondered the reason for a moment, *. . . because we lost our imagination and creative gifts. How did that happen?*

He decided it must be because we gave up on ourselves by thinking we are the top of the so-called food chain. Apex predators. We are far from that.

Merely having talents for talking and solving riddles has sadly separated us from the grander story of nature and the magic of our connection to the cosmos. It is hard to believe that we would choose to look down at a smartphone all day and not upwards to admire the stars in our ever-expanding universe.

We become brain-drained by the noisy nonsense of each day. We exhaust ourselves with the small stuff while the majesty of the infinite universe seems to bore us. Maybe we just can't handle the bigness of it all. He sighed.

He watched a wedge of geese flying across the morning sky. The formation and communication within bird flocks always brought him to silence both in thought and spoken words. Geese and other birds instinctually know how to fly across the sky and where to find sustenance or to rest while they travel from one "home" to another. It befuddled him why all humans do is either watch, ignore, or shoot at geese.

We pretend to understand nature. In reality, we probably only understand maybe a tenth of anything we encounter in the world or our place in it.

But what if we could connect to that which is greater than us, the more, *instead of to the small?* He decides that if we could only make a connection to the infinite, life and death could be seen as a product of our imaginations.

Perhaps the beginning of human life was set at birth and the ending of human life at death purely so we could attribute meaning to the middle. We certainly have created industries around both of those points in human existence. As constructs, we typically allow our beginnings and ends to control the middle part of our days on earth. But there are other ways to define life for ourselves. He thinks, *The narrative about our lives ending with the death of the body seems false to me. Is there a way to break it open?*

Awaiting death was where they found themselves now. The question on the table was: Does it take being on the brink of personal extinction to open up the creative mind, including the brain's subconscious and unconscious modes of cognition, so we can be witnesses to all we were intended to be from the beginning? That was the answer he was struggling to discern.

Whether Shamanism, Sufism, Hinduism, Buddhism, Judaism, or Christianity, or another faith or tradition, all spiritual paths point to us being more than dust after physical life ends. Even if he were to ignore the various religions and philosophies he knew about, what about just acknowledging the fact that he and his wife were energy and wished to rejoin the whole? That was what he wanted.

It is amazing that we have so separated ourselves from the rest of the universe that in death we still believe we will be isolated from Mother Earth and our fellow travelers! The very notion of this limitation was irksome to him.

The idea that we live inside an envelope is our creation. A myth that we allow to define our choices of how we live. The box of options we are permitted is superimposed on us by us! Now it is our moment to dissolve this myth created by man. Why couldn't we join the stars? Why couldn't we break through old myths that keeps us prisoners of a fearful world and create a better myth we either created or have just accepted as our destiny.

The day itself was slowly waking up from its sleep as he watched. He saw a few deer lope into the backyard to graze on the grass. He knew they liked to eat in the morning hours. One of the deer raised its head and seemed to stare at him. The creature blinked and moved its head up and down. They were acknowledging each other. The deer always had felt safe in the backyard at Genesis Road.

He laughed to himself. *If the deer could talk, they could probably explain all that mankind is missing, overlooking, or ignoring. The cures in the grass, the medicine in the plants, the bliss of simply being with family, the beauty of wandering through the woods with no other goal than to wander through the woods. A whole world is here yet a man watches his watch.*

He turned and headed back to the den to finish his letter to Sarah and Rachel.

"The time is getting short now. You may be asking yourself why we didn't include you in this final decision. It is hard to explain. We know you love us. We know you will miss us. We love you more than words can capture. You may think that we will miss watching how your lives and the lives of our grandchildren play out.

"But we truly believe that we will be witnessing all of it. We intend to make our presence known to you, and if you call for us, we will be there in heart, soul, and spirit. To some extent we may be closer to you once we are released from these envelopes to which we find ourselves confined.

"A few final thoughts, my sweet daughters. Don't mourn us. Remember us. Celebrate the good times we have had with each other. Years ago, I read the writings of Dietrich Bonhoeffer. I won't get this exactly right, but I believe that in one of the notes he wrote to his family before his execution by the Nazis he expressed that the debt we owe the dead is to keep on living. Keep on living happy, joyful, productive lives. When you think of us, we hope you smile. We will be watching.

Love, Dad"

He put the pen down, nodded to himself, and then folded the letter and placed it in the envelope. He wrote a few words on the envelope and sealed it. Then he headed to the master bedroom, where he walked into the closet and put the envelope on a ledge.

7. The Beginning

He entered the bedroom and saw his wife sleeping on her side. She had one pillow between her knees and another pillow folded under her head. He did not want to wake her. He sat on the bed and just stared at her. With matted hair, no makeup, and some sweat rolling down her forehead she still looked like the sweet girl he'd met in his youth. Her breathing was shallow. She was so pale and slight. He thought that she had just a few breaths left.

We decided so long ago with whom we wanted to travel this life, he thought. *With whom we wanted to share our lives. Whom we choose. By choosing each other, alternate life stories were never lived.*

Beloved, you never knew where your path would lead you. But it couldn't be helped. You'd made your choice.

Whatever else could have been, the only thing he knew for sure was that he felt grateful that they had both made the choice they had made. And now another choice lay before them.

There are no guarantees about anything in life, especially when it will end. Believing there is an afterlife is a question of faith. But in the end, isn't that all there can be . . . faith?

But maybe there is no beginning or end. Maybe life is an infinite experience. Maybe we cannot fathom the breadth of it all.

She opened her eyes and rolled over onto her back. He helped her sit up in bed. They silently stared at each other.

"I don't have much time," she said. "I feel in every part of me that my life is slipping away. I know I have just a few moments left my love, and I want to thank you for the shared journey. I want to thank you for this life we chose."

"It is not over, my sweet girl," he replied. "It is just the beginning. It is time to call the guide back."

He went into the closet and took out the white robes that they'd brought home years earlier from Istanbul. They were so mesmerized by the whirling dervishes in flowing robes that they'd seen there so they tracked down a shop that sold them. They used to enjoy putting them on and dancing around the house. It just made them smile. But on this day, he was taking out the robes for a different purpose. He wanted them both to be wearing white when they crossed over. He felt there was going to be a connection made between the two of them, the cosmos, and universal consciousness. They were going home. He wanted them to dress in a state of purity.

He dampened a cloth and washed his wife's face with it. He then gently took off her pajamas and dressed her in the white robe. It is the first time he had seen her smile for months. She knew she was going to connect with the more. She was going to be released from the horrid illness and the constant pain that there was no escaping from.

The two of them had spoken for years about the truth that this world is not *the* world. They both refused to believe that man's creation is the whole of Creation. Impossible. They agreed that the intangible world survives the tangible world. How else to explain an undying love? An undying memory? Or the voice that always repeats in your heart and soul which helps you get through the tough moments in life? What else gives you the strength to wake up each day and meet the challenges?

With thoughts like these at the forefront of his mind, he started burning incense. He turned on an audio of a shaman drumming. He dimmed the lights, then lit three candles and sat down on the bed with his wife.

He felt calm. Her presence always had that effect on him. When he was with her, he was in a good place.

His wife was staring at a picture on the wall, the scene of a small boat with two people seated in it floating between limestone karsts in the magnificent Ha Long Bay in Vietnam. He looked at her and then at the picture. He remembered when they were there. It hadn't been long before. They'd cruised through the Bay and then wandered the caves made from the dissolution of rock. *How could you not believe in* more *if you stop and witness the majesty of what is before you? How can you think that it begins and ends when the forever is right before you?* he reflected.

His mind raced to the moment when they first entered Angkor Wat, a mind-numbingly vast twelfth-century temple complex in Cambodia. The largest religious structure in the world, it seemed to stretch into infinity. When there, they found themselves engulfed in a different time and space, "living" outside current time and space. The temple belonged in another world. A real world, but not this world.

As they'd walked the holy grounds, he could hear the voices of those who'd walked the same paths before. Their voices still filled the air all around them both. Wandering the ancient grounds that were still alive with the spirits of those from before had taught him that nothing and no one is ever truly gone.

He thought back to the trees growing around and through the temple structures. What they meant to him were that no matter what a man creates, nature and the universe are always the final arbiters of his existence. *We may foolishly believe that we are somehow the masters of ourselves when in reality we always were and are servants.*

He looked at his wife and asked if she remembered Ha Long Bay and Angkor Wat. She nodded. He touched her hand. "Those ancient sites live on and on," he said. "The souls who lived there still reside there. That is the beauty of believing."

She squeezed his hand in acknowledgment of what she'd heard.

He thought of the Willie Nelson song "Angel Flying Too Close to the Ground." That's who she was to him. He was so grateful she had come to him so long ago and decided to stay. He told her that after that night they would see and speak to each other soul to soul. If there was an angel among the two of them, she clearly was the angel.

He then gave out a short laugh. She asked him what was funny. He explained that from the moment they'd met he had sensed they'd be together forever, and how he wouldn't have it any other way.

He asked his wife to close her eyes while he prayed that Agnam would appear. The room was quiet except for the drumming. He felt like the spirit of people of all faiths from the places they had visited were combining into one. Ruins in Peru, Turkey, Vietnam, Cambodia, Greece, Rome, and the Khumbu region of the Himalayas, the caves of Pech Merle in France, and Indigenous dwellings in Mesa Verde, Colorado.

You couldn't have told him, as they walked through Oradour-sur-Glane, a memorial in France situated where an entire village was massacred by German soldiers in June 1944, that the voices of those lost in time do not still speak and tell each visitor to remember them and live in peace. The world is occupied by the souls of those from history who still have a story to be told, a lesson to be taught, a memory to share. All you need to do to hear these stories is quiet your mind and open your soul.

He could sense the souls of whirling dervishes and ancient shamans joining them in the room to take them both to the upper world, the other side, the awakening, universal consciousness. They were going through an opening to the grander story. It was always there. It is always there . . . waiting for ones willing to let go of ego, let go of the noise, remember, and reconnect.

Once again, they felt a strong presence in the room. The guide was there. From this moment on no outward words would be spoken. There was no chatter. All was silent, except for the drumming in the background.

Agnam opened his arms and gestured for them both to lie down and hold hands. They felt an inner knowing of what to do. They slowed their breathing and began to feel their "outline" dissolving. Whether it was or was not, they could no longer tell. As they felt less in a tangible sense, they felt more in an intangible way. They were entering the world of the infinite. Of the eternal.

The man began to see a cascade of lights and colors. He felt weightless. He couldn't help himself, but he opened his eyes. What he saw, he really couldn't explain. He saw his body dissolving. Not in a scary way. Dissolving in a magical way. It was as if he was now with a masterful magician who had placed him under a cloak and swept it away, and now he was no longer there. Yet his energy, his love for her remained. His vision of his wife was still complete.

There was no fear. There were no frightening visions of life and death. In fact, there was no death. He saw death as an illusion created by man to keep man in his place, so to speak. He saw the universe in all its glory. He was now simply moving from celestial body to celestial body as pure energy. He felt joy like he'd never felt it before.

And then he saw her. His wife was beside him, also traveling through the cosmos. She was ageless, timeless, beautiful. She was pure light. There was no illness now. No disease. Sickness doesn't exist in the universal conscious-ness that they were entering. They nodded to each other as they traveled back and forth in time. It seemed always to be morning wherever they went.

He felt connected to his beloved wife as never before. She squeezed his hand as if she fully understood that they were merely the essence now of what it means to be whole.

At one point during the transition, he looked down and thought he saw the two of them in white robes lying on the bed. Then even that image evaporated.

They felt the guide say that they were now released and could join the ever-expanding universe and witness the lives to come, join the lives that have passed.

He felt himself melting into the fabric of eternity. He was safe. He knew she was too. They were one.

What would happen next he did not know. They were on an adventure that only the ones on it can experience. What the next chapter was he didn't know, and he didn't care. He was with his love.

It was the beginning. It was morning again.

It is always beautiful in the morning.

8. The Letter

Sarah waited for Rachel's flight to arrive so they could drive to the house on Genesis Road together. They had received a police report that no suicide had occurred but were still at a loss to understand exactly what had happened. How could both their parents have died at the exact same moment? They had spoken with their mom just a few days before and tried their best to say all the things they wanted and needed to say. The grandchildren had called and also talked with their grandma. They all cried and told each other how much they each meant to each other. At one point she said, "So, this is what a good life looks and feels like. I am blessed."

They had been speaking with their dad and he told them to be strong. Although he loved them greatly, he did not say anything about his plans for himself. They were frustrated. He did tell them that he had made "notes" that he would share with them.

From a staff member at the funeral home, they had heard that the medical examiner said their mom died of COVID but there was no explainable cause for their dad's death. The most that anyone official could determine was that he'd simply willed himself to join her.

None of it made any sense.

After Rachel touched down and got her suitcase at the luggage carousel, they checked into a hotel and then drove over to the house where they were to meet the realtor in a few hours to discuss what needed to happen—minor improvements—before a sale could go through.

They silently entered their childhood home. It seemed peaceful and empty. They wandered from room to room as memories flooded over them. They each commented that there was no notes from dad anywhere. No letter. No envelope. So many questions were unanswered. But they kept walking through the house.

They smiled as they touched the height lines on the doorframe in the kitchen. Their names and the years of each mark were listed. They hugged.

They sat by the fireplace in the living room and talked for about an hour about all the magical moments that occurred in the house.

Where does a life go when it goes? What happens to the moments of a life? Is it kept in a jar somewhere in the cosmos so we can unlock it from time to time? they wondered.

Sitting in the living room talking about life, the whole experience made no sense to either of them. The whys. The how-comes. The what-ifs. Then they decided to sit outside by the fire pit. They looked out over the field and saw a few deer lope into the backyard almost as if the ruminants were greeting them. Welcoming them to the beginning again.

The realtor came and went. Her requests were to empty the house entirely, add a few coats of fresh paint to the walls, change the lightbulbs, wash the windows, have a gardener tidy up the front and side yards, and repair a couple of broken hinges. The realtor was considering putting the house up for sale in a few weeks once these minor issues were addressed. She wanted the curb appeal to be just right.

While they began putting out trash, the sisters probably talked for hours between jags of crying and laughing. Memories and loss can do that to you. Each had their favorite moments at the house on Genesis Road. They looked at the Mack Truck tire and smiled. "Oh, those afternoons in the summer just swinging and giggling!" said Sarah.

Then the do-you-remember-when talk began. "Remember when Dad did this or when Mom did that? And how we all danced around the living room on our way to the den to 'battle' over pinball wizard challenges?"

They made their way to the master bedroom and just sat on the bed. They wanted to smell everything. Then they made their way into the closet and began to move various hangers of their mom's clothes hanging there. How she loved this or that item. Blue was her favorite color. There were blue clothes everywhere.

They then looked over at their dad's side of the closet and laughed about how every item seemed pretty much the same. Blue, black, and gray tee shirts, jeans, a few sweaters, and a Lone Wolf baseball cap. He was pretty basic in his choices.

Rachel remembered when she bought him that cap. It had just seemed appropriate.

Sarah commented that he'd loved to sit with them when they were little, and how they would make up stories together. They would take turns creating some new part of a story when it was their turn. All the stories seemed to end with little girls, surprisingly named Sarah and Rachel, flying into the sky on some magic carpet or in a hot air balloon.

They then went into the den hoping to find some clues as to the why and how-come of their dad's death. They fingered through some papers on the desk but found nothing that pointed the way to why. *Had he been ill too and never told us?* They opened up the desktop computer, found the username and password, but nothing there explained his demise.

Eventually, the sisters worked their way back to the kitchen and sat on the stools drinking water. They found it almost impossible to fathom that their parents would "leave" them without some note containing a how-come or a let-us-explain message. It made absolutely no sense. They had to be overlooking something.

They then remembered that their dad kept his favorite books on a shelf in the master bedroom closet. So, they headed back there. And there the books were . . . *The Essential Rumi, The Bhagavad Gita, Marcus Aurelius Meditations, The Bible, The Three Worlds of Shamanism, The Tibetan Book of the Dead, The Snow Leopard, My Experiments with Truth* by Gandhi, and *Einstein on Religion.*

They smiled and talked about how their dad was always searching—trying to understand what "any of this" meant. As they thumbed through the books, they noticed a bunch of tee shirts in the corner of the closet on the floor.

Rachel and Sarah went into the garage to see if they could find an empty box in which to put all the tee shirts and other clothes that were either on the floor or on the bed. Sarah grabbed the shirts from the floor and dumped them in the box. She didn't notice that an envelope was wedged between them. She folded up the box cover and tucked the box into a corner of the closet. At least the room looked a bit neater, she felt.

Once the search was done, they decided to grab the sandwiches they'd bought at the airport and eat them in the sun on the deck before heading out. They had much to do.

The women walked out to the wood bridge and sat on the bench next to it. They were both silent. Two butterflies started dancing around them. They just watched them dancing, first around each of them, then between them. A butterfly landed on the arm of each sister. Sarah commented on the bright yellow butterfly that was perched on Rachel's head. Rachel replied that another golden butterfly had moved to Sarah's shoulder. The butterflies did not move. They just stayed there.

Sarah and Rachel finished their snacks and were going to walk around the house one more time before calling it a day. They knew they would be back the next morning to start the deeper, more arduous task of organizing and packing their parents' possessions, and figuring out what to do with them.

As they entered the house, the butterflies remained sitting on their respective shoulders and heads. The girls didn't mind.

Once inside, the butterflies took flight. Sarah and Rachel decided that they would go get the butterflies and "escort" them safely to the outside, so they propped open the back door, creating an exit for the insects, then followed the butteries through the house, ending up in the master bedroom closet.

The girls watched as both butterflies landed on the closed box of their father's clothing. They would not budge from it on their own.

Sarah and Rachel looked at each other and almost in unison said, "Are they trying to tell us something?"

Sarah suggested, "Let's open the box and see what the different tee shirts say on them. Maybe there is a message we need to see on one of the shirts."

Rachel dragged the box out of the closet and across the floor to the bed, then placed it on the mattress. The butterflies followed them. Their behavior was just so beautifully strange. She laughed and asked, "Mom, is that you?"

Together they reopened the box and pulled out the whole stack of tee shirts and unfolded several. And there it was . . . the envelope fell to the floor. Sarah picked it up and read the writing on the outside of the envelope aloud, "Reflections and random thoughts," then held it out to show it to her sister. Recognizing the handwriting, both women nodded and simultaneously commented, "Dad."

The envelope was taped shut. Sarah carefully peeled the tape off and slowly opened the back flap, revealing a folded-up letter. It had to be twenty pages long or more. They took it and walked with it into the living room.

Sarah said she was too nervous to read it. Rachel said she would read it out loud. She unfolded the letter and began. As if guided by the sound of her voice, the butterflies flew out through the back door and vanished into the field in the backyard.

The family was all back together again at the house on Genesis Road.

Epilogue

After a few weeks of working to clean up the house and get it ready for sale, Rachel and Sarah spoke about how much they loved Genesis. They had found out that there was no mortgage on the property; their parents had owned it free and clear. The estate lawyer told them that after all probate proceedings were done the two of them would own it equally and could do whatever they wanted with it.

They had long talks with their husbands and kids about how much they loved the house, the land, and the history of this unique place. They explained that Genesis was magical, and they felt the presence of their mom and dad there, especially on the deck looking over the mountain range. And oh, those butterflies! They loved it all so much!

An agreement was reached. The sisters would keep Genesis in the family and it would be their joint vacation, retreat, holiday, gathering spot for all time.

They pulled the listing off the market.

They had a butterfly pavilion constructed by the bridge over the dry riverbed.

The house on Genesis Road was again home to the entire family.

Acknowledgments

When COVID took over life as we know it, destroying so many families, it hit my family too. It took the life of Brad, the husband of my daughter Lindsay, and the heartache we all felt was immeasurable. Both Lindsay and my grandson Hunter were brave and helped each other and the rest of us navigate the brutal terrain of loss. This immense tragedy was the trigger for the writing of *The House on Genesis Road,* which is my effort to make sense of experiences in life that can't be made sense of. I see the book as a story of everlasting love and hope in a world that needs it more than ever.

I want to thank my wife, Margie, who is my rock and the glue and spine of our family. And I want to thank my daughters, Melissa and Lindsay, for always showing resilience, love, and courage in the most tragic of times, and my son-in-law, Mason, for his friendship to me. I also want to thank my grandchildren, Ryan, Reghan, and Hunter for illuminating the brighter future to come.

In addition, I want to thank my friends who have encouraged me to write about my life experiences and always give me hope for a better tomorrow.

I am grateful to my book editor, Stephanie Gunning, for making this work better at every turn; and to you, my dear reader: I hope you have found a measure of peace by taking your journey through *The House on Genesis Road.*

ABOUT THE AUTHOR

Paul R. Lipton is a devoted husband, father, and grandfather, and the author of three books of which *The House on Genesis Road* is the third. The others are *Hour of the Wolf: An Experiment in Ageless Living* and the novel *In These Five Breaths.* A longtime resident of Florida, Paul now lives with his wife, Margie, in Longmont, Colorado.

www.ingramcontent.com/pod-product-compliance
Lightning Source LLC
Chambersburg PA
CBHW060331260626
47160CB00007B/2773